SKINNY, Dippin'

By Didi Oviatt

ACKNOWLEDGMENTS

A SPECIAL THANK YOU to each and every one of the 17 extremely talented authors who took part in the original SINNERS & SAINTS anthology. Getting to know and work with you was a real pleasure!

CHAPTER 1

I SLAM MY car door a little too hard. I can't believe I'm actually considering my kids' nonsense extended vacation proposition. They've been talking about my taking some much-needed time to myself for a couple of years now, but to seriously go and approach my boss behind my back, what gall. I don't know whether to smack them each, or to hug their guts out for caring so much about their aging mom.

It's bad enough that I have to see my ex-husband running around with some tramp who's only five years older than our kids -- with her perky boobs, and tight thighs -- buying her new dresses and taking her out to all the fancy places. Okay, I've only actually seen her once, and she was really nice to me. She's nice to my kids, too. She and Marsha even share shoes. But I have spies who fill me in on her dirt and I'll cling to every curse word she's been caught saying in public. To top off everything out of my hands, my kids are getting serious about forcing me to live in a beachside condo for an entire summer. What is my life coming to?

I sigh and pop the trunk before reaching in for the single paper sack of groceries. It's stuffed to the brim, enough to throw together a less than ideal Friday night dinner for my twin meddlers. I wrestle it into the crook of my arm. The kids asked for steak, I'll give them spaghetti. Paybacks for their intrusion on my otherwise uneventful day. Everything was going just fine and dandy before Mark, my boss, pulled me into his office the very second I closed my till.

I packed up the last of my things, leaving my paperwork organized in a nice and tidy stack by my nameplate. It merely reads **Carla**. Mine is the only nameplate without a last name at this bank. Seven years ago, when I divorced, I kept my husband's name so that I'd forever be the same as my children. That doesn't mean I need to advertise it. Asking Mark to order me a new plate was among the first changes I made.

It's rare for him to call any of us tellers into his office at closing time. I could count on both hands just how many times in the last fifteen years this has happened.

"I had an interesting chat with your kids this afternoon while you were at lunch," he said.

My stomach sank as I reeled over what they could possibly want with my boss.

"Oh God," I'd replied. "Together those two are the devil himself. Don't listen to a word they tell you... ever."

Mark only laughed at my response and told me that he agrees with their devious ways one hundred percent. Apparently Suzanne, our usual call-in at First National, will be packing up her things and attending college in a different state by the end of the summer, and has been begging for a full-time position at our branch - just until she moves. Taking over my shift while I'm on leave would benefit her immensely, and I have plenty of money put away to cover my living expenses.

Marsha and Dean even told Mark all about their intentions to hold the fort down at my home. They talked to him about my love life, or lack of, and the potential of my finding a mate on the beach. Nothing is sacred around here, and my boss found their entire approach to be like a hilarious game of chess where I'm the pawn. They've covered every angle and detail imaginable. Talk about an awkward and inappropriate conversation to be having with my boss. Thanks kids!

Mark went on to tell me that an extended personal leave wasn't completely out of the question. All jokes aside, he encouraged my taking a bold move at self-improvement, despite my argument that too much sun isn't exactly good for people. Then he went ahead and dropped the guilt bomb.

"Carla," he tilted himself forward, folding his arms on his desk and closing a little distance between our faces. "I spent the entire afternoon back and forth on the phone with Danika, the HR personnel officer from the central office up state."

I deflated. "You didn't."

"I sure did, and she pulled up your file to review it for a pre-approval of an extended personal leave. In fifteen years, you've only taken off twenty personal days. You've trained dozens of other tellers who have come and gone, and you've capped on pay raise dividends twice. Danika agreed with me that you're very deserving of a personal leave, especially since

Suzanne is ready and willing to slide into your shift while you're gone. Apparently, not needing to hire and train anyone to fill your shoes is a big selling factor for the board. She already started all the necessary paperwork on her end."

"I can't believe this is happening," I mumbled and pinched the skin between my eyes with my thumb and pointer.

He went on to show me the stack of paperwork that would need to be filled out by me and signed by the both of us. As acting branch manager, he's already emailed a formal letter of personal leave recommendation, as his approval is the first step, followed by Danika, followed by the board. Danika didn't doubt for a second that the board would give it a stamp of approval. She even offered to address it personally during a meeting they'll all be attending at the beginning of next week.

He handed me a short stack of pages, already printed off with my name on them, just waiting for me to fill in the blanks. Vaguely, if at all possible, and to state in writing that the reason for a leave request is, "of personal family business," as per Danika's recommendation.

"Carla, you never even took time off with your divorce," he said, "and your kids are in their twenties now. You're one hell of an employee, and your job isn't going anywhere. If there is anyone here who deserves a break, it's you."

"Maybe I've never taken time off because maintaining a mundane lifestyle is the only thing that keeps me sane," I teased.

"Don't make my entire afternoon a waste, Carla." He leaned back in his chair and clamped his hands behind his head. "Sounds like your kids have all the details covered. What were the words Marsha used? You're growing stagnant?" He grinned from ear to ear with amusement. "If all goes smooth with the board, we could have you checked out by the end of next week."

"But today's Friday."

"Yep."

"Why do I get the feeling you're all trying to get rid of me?"

To that he only chuckled and sent me on my way. On the drive home I passed the same billboard that I do every day, only this time I truly looked at it. A young man on the beach. His naked back, dripping with ocean water accentuating every muscle – clear down to the tag of his underwear, that's meant to be advertised. What would it be like to run my fingers across the shoulder line of a man that fit? If the front of him matched the back of him, I'd probably even give the sweat on his stomach a lick. *Maybe a summer on the beach isn't such a bad idea after all.*

Despite my inner turmoil leaning toward defeat, here I am, preparing to stand my ground against my kids over some fraction of a chance at change, at hope, at adventure. A chance that I never got after marrying too young and dedicating myself entirely to raising them. I don't regret a second of the way I've brought up my children, but now that they're grown, I think I'm losing my mind. My thoughts are everywhere. I'm scattered, and they can tell.

I'm scared to death of what my life will be when they finish college. Maybe a break *is* what I need. A slow transition to my being alone, all the while I know they're still safe at home. Then again, maybe Marsha and Dean really just want my house to themselves. I'm clinging to every last second I have with them, and they want to ship me off. It's weird, yet for some reason my gut is telling me to go for it. The two of them are the most dramatically persistent humans on the planet. I suppose I should be proud. They're destined to accomplish big things, both of them. Once they put their minds to something there's no limit to the lengths they'll go.

On the money side of things, I really lucked out with my kids' scholarships. The funds I had saved for their schooling wasn't needed so it continues to accumulate interest, and the two of them are refusing to spend it on anything but "family wellness." Whatever the hell that's supposed to mean. I keep waiting for either one of them to let their selfishness shine through, but it's yet to happen. They're great kids, so I can't imagine them to have ill intentions. But, why now?

Damn it, Carla, stop overthinking!

Slowly, the air releases from my lungs and I stomp my feet to the house. The paperwork for my leave sits perfectly concealed on the front seat of my car. The last thing I want is to have my kids see them right off the bat. I pull a stalk of celery out of the overstuffed paper bag in one hand, so I can point it at my children while I make my way into the kitchen.

"Mom!" Dean throws his hands in the air, palms toward me in surrender. "Before you say anything, just hear us out."

"You're a villain," I say and thrust the celery around like a sword. I wave it back and forth between them. "Both of you."

"Disarm yourself, Woman." Marsha chimes in.

"We only did what we had to. You never would've taken the initiative at work if we didn't step in. There's only so long you can use your job as an excuse."

She rounds the bar to take the awkwardly full paper bag from my arm and sets it next to the stove before the bottom has a chance to give way and spill its grocery guts all over the tiled floor. She's completely unfazed by my foodish threats and doesn't even glance in the celery's direction.

Dean's face lights up at my lighthearted humor. With wide eyes he laughs openly, then he shakes his head and returns his attention back to the schoolwork in front of him. Finals are rapidly approaching, so they've both been glued to their studies. It's been peaceful this last week, but a little lonely I'll admit. Another reason I'm afraid to be by myself for the summer. I'm a great mom, and for the most part my kids prefer to spend the majority of their time with me, so I'm rarely lonely.

I don't want to be alone for months on end. My mind wanders to the billboard, and I remind myself of the water dripping down the muscular back. Okay, alone is one thing. Alone on the beach might not be so bad, with the possibility of a view like that close by.

"Spaghetti? Really?" Marsha moans, pulling the sauce from the bag and holding it into the air with her other hand on her hip. One brow slowly lifts to a perfectly pointed form of quizzical defiance. Her brows are the best, it's like they each work on their own grid. Separate entities and such. "I thought we were having steak. Do you realize we requested it by way of celebration?"

"I don't take requests from traitors." I tell her and

take a dramatic crunch from the end of my celery stalk.

Dean cringes. Without looking up he mumbles, "You know you didn't wash that, right?"

I shrug, "I guess if I die of an unclean veggie disease then I won't have to leave work for three months to live in a stranger's house then, huh?"

Marsha talks over her shoulder while she fills a pot of water to boil the noodles in.

"Mom you know Stephany, she's far from a stranger. Her family needs someone they can trust to stay in their house for the summer. We've gone over this. The plants need watering, squatters kept at bay, the dust needs to not accumulate... blah blah blah. It's a really nice place, Mom. It's only two hours away, and it's right on the beach."

"I'm forty-one years old. I don't need a summer on the beach. I need a warm fuzzy blanket, a *How to Knit for Dummies* book, and the cure to cottage cheese ass."

"Gross!" Dean interjects.

I lean my rear end against the fridge and cross one foot over the other while I continue to munch on my uncleansed food. If nothing else, I'll kick back and let Marsha prep dinner while I whine in protest. Dean has textbooks and notes splayed out across the entire kitchen table. He's completely buried in his studies. I'm surprised he had the capability of noticing my food, or my ass comments. He's always been a one-track-mind kind of guy, and despite his usually carefree humor, he's determined to make it into medical school.

"Whatever." Marsha says. She pulls out a chopping block and sets to work on a salad. "You don't have any sign of cottage cheese ass. You're a devilishly hot middle-aged woman with perfect skin and minimal wrinkles."

"Why thank you, my dear meddler."

Crunch, the last bite of celery rolls around on my tongue.

"Really though," she persists, "the beach is just what you need. Show off that body of yours while you still can. Time is ticking you know."

I roll my eyes dramatically and flop myself down on a barstool. Drumming my fingers on the countertop gives me a fidgeting outlet while I watch my daughter take over dinner with ease, moving from dish to pot, careful not to over-season or over-cook anything. She's always so comfortable in the kitchen. I don't know where she gets it. I'm certainly no chef, and the only thing her father's ever managed to do is burn a few BBQ's. Thank God for the sexy pizza delivery guy who comes around with our usual at least once a week. Maybe I like pizza, maybe I like his smile - who knows.

"Okay," I announce, "let's toy with the idea that I go along with this summer plot."

Everything stills. Marsha stops stirring the sauce and stands like a statue. No breathing, no moving, only holding as stiff as humanly possible as she waits for me to continue. Dean looks up from his studies with his mouth agape. I chuckle and keep talking.

"Let's say we use up a bit of *your* saving accounts." I accentuate the word your, to really drive my point home. "Then what? Dean, how will you be able to afford a fancy new sports car? Marsha, what if you decide you want to rebel a little? You know, buy a bunch of expensive clothes, cover half your body in tattoos, get a boob job?"

"Arrrrgh," Dean moans, and without looking up he reminds me. "I'm going to be a doctor soon, remember? By the time I go through a midlife crisis and want a flashy car, I'll be able to afford two."

Marsha taps the sauce off of her stirring spoon before setting it down and spinning on her heels to face me.

"A boob job? Really? That's your argument?"

I shrug and wait for her inevitable rant.

"For starters," she says, "don't make things awkward. You know I like having small boobs, it's the cool thing these days, natural and all. Plus, I have a tiny frame like yours, big boobs would just make me look... weird. Besides that, we agreed to split your spending money between the two of us. We'll each keep an eye on your account and fill it up as needed." Her toothy smile rings proud. "Easy peasy. We're not worried about you spending it all. We know you better!"

"You might change your mind on the boobs." I argue. "Plus, I'm the mom here, remember?"

Dean starts cleaning up his mess, stacking and organizing papers before sliding them into their rightful folders and slamming all of his books shut.

"Mom," he says. "Just cut to the chase. Why are you fighting this? It's the last summer Stephany's family will need a house sitter, like probably ever. They don't want anyone they're unsure of or that they can't trust, so you're a perfect fit. Stephany has convinced them not to find anyone else until you make up your mind. They're leaving next week, and you'll never find an opportunity like this again."

"Maybe it's because I, well, I'm old."

"No, you're not." He argues.

I ponder his straightforward approach. "Too old to run off and spend a summer on the beach. It's strange. What am I supposed to do with myself? Swim?"

In unison they blurt, "Maybe you'll meet someone."

"I knew it!" I shout, drop my head back, and throw my palms in the air. "I knew that's what this was all about. You two just assume that a single woman on the beach automatically summons a hook-up of sorts. Not every aging lady needs a man, you know."

With that, my stomach knots. I haven't been with a soul since I divorced Bradley and hadn't fooled around with him for at least two years before that. The dirty cheater. Anyway. I'm not exactly sure how long it's been since I got laid. Depressing, I know. Some say that with time, the ache for human touch goes away. That's a bold-faced lie in my case. I think about sex all the time, and it only grows with age. I miss it. At one point I was even good at it. No... great at it.

All my friends have tried hooking me up on blind dates, insisting that orgasms are top notch when you're in your thirties. It never panned out. I hated all the dates and didn't even let them get to second base. I guess the whole, "sex is amazing in your mid-to-late thirties" myth will forever remain a mystery for me. Perhaps this summer I'll find out how things work in bed for an early forties gal?

Marsha dishes me a plate before helping herself and joining me at a bar stool followed by Dean. We eat in comfortable silence for most of the meal, with an occasional mention of Dean's nerves about finals. Marsha doesn't bat an eye at test time, never has.

Unique is the best way to describe my yoga loving munchkin. She'll throw herself into a pretzel for an extra thirty minutes over her normal routine on test days, quoting all of her notes between deep breaths. Then she trots off to school and aces every essay and test that comes her way. With a grin on her face she comes home from school and helps herself to a single glass of my wine to celebrate. Then she moves along with life as if no stress can possibly penetrate her. She's done this since ninth grade, and I kept my mouth shut about the single glass of wine. If that's her process, then it's worked. One glass never hurt any-one, and she's otherwise a saint.

They know that I'm thinking seriously about the summer condo, or they wouldn't have talked to my boss in the first place. Overstepping boundaries is a common thing in our family, but only because I've en-couraged them since birth to take fearless steps when the outcome is for the greater good and no one can possibly get hurt in the process. Bold approaches are a learning experience. That's what I've always told them, and now it's backfired against me. They don't push the subject, for now. I mostly contemplate every possible scenario with each slurp of a noodle. Over analyzing is an issue for me, one that I've embraced at my age.

A two-hour drive isn't too far away from my kids. I could come home to see them whenever I want, or vice-versa. They promised to come out on a few week-ends here and there, or on days that there's no school. It's logical, and any middle-class single woman who's spent her entire life living in the same town would be mad not to jump on such an opportunity. I could use the time to relax, sleep in and even read.

I have three whole bookshelves full of paperbacks that I haven't touched since I swiped my debit card for their purchase. Call me silly but I buy more books than I could possibly read. Always have, and likely always will. Some women like to spend their extra cash on pretty accessories, like purses and belts. I like beautiful paperbacks with the promise of an adventure worth their design printed on the back. Fortunately for me there are hundreds of books granting such promise, practically everywhere I look.

Inevitably my mind wanders back to the possibility of meeting someone. What if I actually did meet a man? What would I do with myself? What if I forgot how it all works down there? What if I get too wet? Or worse... too dry? Oh my God, what if men have evolved and gotten bigger all the while my vagina has shrunk from non-usage and he can't get it in? I snort out loud at the thought, trying to hold back a laugh. It causes my kids to eye me with suspicion. I wave a hand of dismissal in their direction and swallow my last bite of garlic bread.

Of course you'd know what to do, Carla, you're a rockstar in the sack, I correct my own inner battle with a necessary and likely accurate compliment, as all women should.

"Thanks for the dinner, Marsha." I've practically licked my plate clean. "It was good!"

She raises one brow at me again. This time the left one and forms a purse of her lips to accompany it.

"Coulda been steak," Dean pipes up, clearly speaking on behalf of his sister's facial expression.

"Yeah yeah," I say. "I liked it!"

"Annnnnd?" Marsha pushes me to continue.

"And..." I take a deep breath and talk as fast as my tongue will allow. "One of you can find a movie to rent, I'll buy, and the other is welcome to book a couple rooms in Cayucos on my credit card for tomorrow night. If I'm going to house-sit for a summer, then I'd better go meet its owners before they leave."

"YES!" Marsha shouts while Dean does a celebratory fist pump into the air. She jumps from her seat. "Mom, you're going to have SO much fun! And--"

"Stop!" I interject with a palm an inch from her face. "Don't get too excited! If I get a bad feeling about anything at all while I'm there, then I'm backing out."

"You won't," she beams. "You'll love the condo, AND the beach, AND--"

"Stop!" I interrupt again. "Just go book the rooms and shut up before I change my mind. And pack your shit too, both of you. You're coming with."

CHAPTER 2

BREAKFAST IS MY favorite. Well, it's my favorite *after* I've had a good twenty minutes of alone time, locked away in my room with a gigantic cup of coffee. Dean got me an oversized mug for a Christmas gift nearly a decade ago. It's plastered with close-up pictures of him and Marsha pulling ridiculously embarrassing faces, and it literally holds over half a pot of coffee. He thought it was a funny gag gift at the time, but little did he know I'd cling to it forever. Like a life source, feeding me just the right amount of caffeine to pull me out of zombie mode in the mornings.

Today I hold onto it tightly while the very outer cushion of my rear sits on the edge of a signature bench. It hugs the bottom of my bed, a perfect fit. It's my favorite piece of furniture in the entire house. I bought it as a reading bench, but I usually only use it as a quiet and grounding place to align my chakras and enjoy coffee. My eyes are wide and I'm rocking back and forth slightly, keeping the motion alive with the tips of my toes on the carpet.

Marsha attempted to walk in and talk to me at

one point, only to take one look at my face and back away slowly, exactly like one would a bear in the wild. I'm pretty sure she even did it on the tips of her toes. Not completely positive though, it was hard to tell in my peripheral as my eyes were glued to a dirty spot on the wall. She had a handful of bikini tops draped over her forearm, likely wanting my opinion on today's attire.

I've assumed this position for a good twenty minutes now, so I suppose it's time to pull myself out of it. I'm not even nervous about seeing the condo and meeting Stephany's parents, that's the weird part. I've spoken to them on the phone plenty, our children have been close for years and we have much in common. I feel like I'm exactly where I need to be, and doing exactly what I need to do, oddly enough. What's got me spacing out on a dirt spot and rocking myself to a dark blend this morning is the aftermath of the dream I woke up to.

There was a little girl. She had a gigantic sun hat on, so I didn't get a very good look at her face, but she couldn't have been older than five. She was sitting on a beach chair, kicked back with her bare feet crossed at the ankles and the paint on her toes was a bubblegum pink. I was sitting in a similar chair right next to her, sipping a margarita. The breeze was as welcome as the sun that was beating down on us, and I was consumed by comfort. It was natural, sitting there just the two of us. It felt like I'd known her her whole life. That is, until she reached her tiny hand over to place it on mine.

In her sugar-coated voice, she called me, "C-ma."

I'd jolted awake, sitting straight up in a cold sweat. My first thought was Marsha, but how could that possibly be? She tells me everything. Even the silly things like how Rigdon from science class in tenth grade slipped her the tongue. It made her gag because he had too much spit in his mouth, and he tasted like an onion sandwich. He was mortified at her response to him, and she never talked to him again. My dreams have never lied about the serious stuff, though. They're strange like that.

Aside from the farfetched dreams, like flying and making random animal friends, I have this odd way of telling if the emotions in them are genuine... if they're rooted in reality. I don't like to call it a premonition, I'm not a psychic by no means. However, I dreamt of my twins, my brother's car crash, my wedding dress. Hell, I even dreamt of the exact girlfriend Bradley had while we were married, all the way down to her siren hair and shoulder freckles.

Why would this little girl call me C'ma rather than Grammy, or even straight up Grandma? I can't for the life of me figure it out. My own kids called their grandmas GramGram, surely they'd carry on the tradition. Maybe it isn't one of my kids', maybe a friend's? No, it doesn't feel like she belonged to a friend. She felt too close in the dream, like she was mine. Oh shit, maybe I should be on birth control this summer. No, I'm too old. But am I? Having a child at forty-one isn't completely unheard of. I haven't started menopause yet after all.

Trying to wrap my head around the dream has every part of me on edge. Heat, I need heat. I'll steam the flesh bumps away in a long hot shower. Whatever swimsuit issue Marsha is having can wait. I need to relax my muscles and clear my head. It was just a dream after all, can't be real, can't be my kids. Even though a growing baby bump would be the perfect reason behind wanting to ship me off for the summer.

Stop it, Carla, pull yourself together! Even if that little girl was one of your kid's children, she might not make an appearance for years to come! Stop obsessing!

I take a deep breath and count to five before letting it out slowly. Shower, I'm most definitely in need of a shower. I pull myself to my feet and lock the door to my bedroom on auto pilot, separate from any conscious thought process. I leave the door to the master bathroom open so that the steam can escape into my room.

I plug my Bluetooth speaker into the power outlet before undressing. I wouldn't want the speaker's battery life to die a premature death. Music is my center, my chi. I like all kinds. My playlists are impressive, and they're lumped into dozens of categories ranging from year, to artist, to genre, to mood, to pace, and more. This morning I need something calming, something with a little simplicity on life's perspective. I need a smooth voice and a mellow beat. By the end of my shower I want to be able to take charge of the day confidently. I want to enjoy a road trip with my kids without constantly questioning their motives... or reproductive systems for that matter.

Simplicity, comfort, and confidence, that's what I need.

I find a slow-moving eighties list; that ought to help push away the dream. It might even help me find a way to melt my insecurities, the ones I keep tucked inside. Being single has long ago given me the chance to throw all reason out the window. I'm allowed to dance around making a fool of myself and play dress up in public with my children - without batting an eye of embarrassment. I'm comfortable with bold out-takes and sarcasm. But the truth is, I'm not okay at all with the fact that I'm finally showing signs of aging in my face and body. I'm a young forty-one, there's no arguing that. But the crow's feet around my eyes are forming, and I'm getting some of that loose skin under my biceps when I lift my arms. It sucks, and I fear that if I don't find someone who loves me for me now, then I might not ever.

Cayucos is a fairly small beach town in Cali. It's tucked away on a gorgeous hillside with a pier to die for. It's a beautiful place and it's quiet, full of mostly locals. It isn't a busy tourist city, or a teenage hormone fest. My kids weren't lying when they told me it'd be a quiet escape, the kind of city that's a fit for all ages. There's even charming antique shops with the promise of finding old books that I can wrap my heart around.

I scrub the shampoo into my scalp extra hard and take deep breaths in the relaxing steam. The muscles in my back absorb the heat while I stretch my arms and neck every which way. After a good fifteen min-utes or longer of clearing my head, I watch the last of my soap bubbles disappear down the drain. "Free Fallin'" blares through the speaker, appropriate. I've managed to place that little girl from my dream on the back burner of my mind. If something is going on in the baby department with my kids, they'll tell me when they're ready, and I'll embrace it. If it's me who's meant to bring another life into the world... well we'll just cross that bridge when, no *if*, it gets here.

I choose a quirky summer dress with pineapples on it. Then I twist a little chunk of my long brunette hair on top on my head, leaving a spike of ends to peak out at the side. Makes me look young and saucy, I like it. I skip down the hall and into the kitchen where the scent of waffles is filling the air in swirls of awesomeness.

Dean's cramming in one last study session at the kitchen counter before our spur of the moment trip. He likely set an alarm and has been at it for hours, bless his heart. Marsha's whisking away at a fluffy blend of something strawberry and cream cheese-y for a topping. She has her back to me and is swaying her hips to the beat of whatever song she's got plugged into her earbuds. Kids after my own music-loving heart, the both of them. She's oblivious to her surroundings, so naturally I plan to act on it.

Dean looks up to see my placing a shush finger over my lips, he narrows his eyes mischievously and nods me in her direction. He's giving me an encouraging go ahead on my devious endeavors. I bob my head up and down in agreement and slowly, silently, I creep toward her. I close in the distance and in a flash, I grab her with the tips of each finger at the rib cage and shout, "BAH!" at the top of my lungs to the back of her head.

She jumps, arms flailing about and it causes the wire whisk to fly across the room. It lands right in the middle of Dean's textbook. Marsha spins around to scowl and places a hand on her rapidly beating heart. I have to grip the countertop to stop myself from falling over in laughter. The look on her face is absolutely priceless.

Dean groans and grunts between unstoppable giggles while he peels the whisk from his page. Some of the topping drips back down to it with a *thud*. The vivid image he's studying is the anatomy of a full-bodied man, and it's now splotched with a pinkish colored goo.

"Shit," he says and continues to laugh. "Now what am I supposed to do?"

I can't even answer, I'm still doubled over. I can't look at Marsha either, with her flared nostrils and pointed brows.

"Aww," I sigh and catch my breath. "You should see your face."

Marsha pulls the earbuds away from her head and shoves them into her short, cut-off jeans pocket. Then she wipes away the single chunk of creamy topping that splashed onto her forehead.

"Glad to see that blaring 80's rock to the point of busting out windows has brightened your spirits this morning."

"Yep," I agree. "Me too! Good choice on waffles, smells amazing."

"Yeah." The sides of her mouth play at a smile, but only for a second before retreating to a tight-lipped scowl. "Really though. When I went into your room this morning, you looked like death warmed over. Are you okay?"

"I think so, yeah."

I grab a towel and toss it to Dean, who's still staring at his now wet and sticky book page. "I just had a weird dream, that's all. Let's not talk about it. Did you get your swimsuit dilemma straightened out?"

With that, that whole morning is right back on track. We eat, we joke around about the naked, cream covered man in Dean's book as it sits in the corner with its pages splayed out to dry; a fan of shame. We even go over a quick mental checklist with one another about everything we have packed for the trip. My kids spend their usual amount of time texting friends while I tidy up the kitchen. No sooner than I press the start button on the dishwasher, my doorbell rings.

"Oh," Dean chimes in. "I forgot to mention that I invited a friend along."

Marsha and I stare at him blankly.

"What do you mean, you forgot?" I ask. "That's kind of a big invitation, isn't it?"

"Yeah," Marsha agrees. "Please don't tell me I have to get hit on by one of your friends for two whole days! Maybe I should go switch out the swimsuits that I packed to one-pieces — better yet, full-body snorkel gear."

He tilts his head to the side and cuts her an annoyed glower with his hands on his hips. The doorbell rings again and none of us are in any hurry to answer it.

"If she was just a friend, she would have walked in by now," he says.

"Wait... she?" I ask. "How long have you been seeing this one?"

I hold my breath, trying my darndest not to think of my dream. Dean goes through girls like weekly specials at a mom and pop diner. I'd worry more about the dream baby being his, but I genuinely believe that he doesn't actually sleep with them.

I know he's telling the truth about it, because he's always testing them in innocent yet tedious ways He gives them weird and sometimes embarrassing tasks just to see if they're up for the challenge. Plus, he talks in his sleep. He sleep-told me not too long ago that he's only slept with two girls since he's been in college and he regretted it because they both stalked him afterwards. He said that now he 'wants to be sure.' Even more proof that they're good enough kids to leave behind in my home for an entire summer.

When they were in high school, Marsha and I spent a large amount of time making Dean watch boring shows with us. Ones that would inevitably put him to sleep on the couch. Then we'd shut down the television and turn all the lights off to keep him comfortable, so that we could eat popcorn and ask him random questions while he slept. That kid would spill the beans about every detail of his life; nothing is ever a secret when Dean's snoozing. He's handsome too, and I don't just say that because he's my son. He's like a confident Ryan Gosling, abs and all. The girls just keep running at him.

Dean shrugs at my question and grins. "Since today." Then he chuckles. "I think she'll be fun. It's promising. You'll like her."

He turns for the living room with a single bounce to his step. Poor girl, she's doomed. I let the air out of my lungs and shake my head in awe of him. I swear that kid never ceases to surprise me. I nudge Marsha in the arm, and she only pulls her shoulders up toward her ears and mouths a silent, *I don't know.* We're standing in the middle of the room, no direction, no purpose, just listening like inexperienced spies. I can't make out what they're saying, but her voice sounds young, too young. I pull my brows together and look at Marsha out of the corner of my eye, only to see that she's doing the same. Their voices grow closer and we kind of panic.

Scrambling for a place to stand, or something to

hold in our hands that might make us look cool and natural, we fail miserably, both of us. We're standing too close together, so finding a common ground amidst sudden panic of being caught eavesdropping is impossible.

Dean rounds the corner with a cute young girl who has flowing brunette curls, just as Marsha and I ram into one another at full force. Our faces crash together. My nose nearly takes out her eyeball.

Marsha clutches her eye with both hands, folds herself forward at the waist and shouts, "Damn it!"

Dean laughs. "Guys, this is Tina, she's in my Biochemistry class."

"Hi!" she says, very chipper. "Dean told me all about you. I'm excited to see what surprises are up his sleeve."

Spoken like a willing and capable candidate, up to the challenge that is everything Dean. She has a carry-on sized luggage bag on wheels, likely full of clothing and necessities. She also has a large purse, it's a cute one with fringe. I like her taste. What I don't understand is the huge duffle bag tossed over her shoulder. All in all, this Tina chick has brought more stuff than the three of us combined. I notice the ever-growing grin on Dean's face as he watches me size her up. Marsha gains her composure and gives her a wave as if they've already met. Likely in school, but I don't ask.

I clear the lump in my throat. "Nice to meet you, Tina. I'm Dean's mom, Carla."

"What's in the bag?" Marsha asks.

"Oh, these are props," she smiles. "Dean didn't tell me what we were doing. He just said to bring lots of props, a swimsuit, toothbrush and Pjs." She looks up, and out the corner of her eye as if she's trying to recall anything she may have missed. "There might have been more, I don't remember."

A proud grin takes over Tina's face, and I see it. That light -- the bold and adventurous tendencies of the exact type of woman Dean is after. Tina has it, sparkling boldly in her excited eyeballs. Hopefully Dean didn't see it too. I'm sure he has before though. Shit, no wonder he said she has promise.

Dean flashes her his most confident and mischievous grin.

Don't think about the dream. Don't think about the dream.

"So?" he questions, leaning against his elbow on the counter. "What props did you bring?"

Tina doesn't even ask what they're needed for. She heaves it off of her shoulder and onto the freshly cleaned countertop with a clunking *thud*, and then unzips it all the way from one end to the other.

Her arms circle the air as far as she can reach. "Ta-Da!" She says. "Help yourself. It's the best I could do on short notice. An hour didn't give me much time to gather anything more than some random stuff I had laying around."

"Wait a minute," Marsha says, as she digs around in the bag. "Dean invited you an hour ago?"

"Yep," he chuckles. "I texted her right after you two massacred my textbook with waffle topping."

Tina giggles. It has a soft, sing-song ring to it. She doesn't ask questions, only enjoys the moment, and pulls a top hat out of the bag to place on Dean's head. He follows suit and rummages around until he finds a matching corn-cob pipe. He holds it out to her, and she bites down on the small end, accepting the offer.

Marsha and I watch them, absorbing their comfort with one another as he pulls his phone out of his pocket and snaps a selfie. They each pull a face to match their props. Her with one hand holding the pipe to her lips, and the other hand scratching at some non-existent chin stubble. Dean gives his phone a wink and a slight lift of the hat. It *is* an adorable picture; she's definitely doomed.

"How is it that you just have this stuff laying around, anyway?" he questions. "I really didn't think you'd pull off a bag of props." His smile grows even wider, as if that's possible.

Tina shrugs. "I like Halloween and playing dress up." She says that as if she isn't a grown woman at all, but a very confident and precise young girl on her way to Disney on Ice. "Next time, it's my turn to give you an impossible task. Let's see if you're as great at it as I am."

"I will be," he retorts.

Marsha pulls a few large-and-in-charge floppy sun hats from the bag and holds them between her upper arm and ribcage. Then she digs around a little more until she comes across a Ziplock bag full of plastic disco jewelry and gigantic sunglasses.

"Well, I'm ready," she says. "Let's get this show on the road, shall we?"

CHAPTER 3

THE MAN ON the billboard that I pass every day going to and from work practically jumps off of his gigantic perch and kisses me right on the face on our way out of town. That muscular back on the beach is my first confirmation that making this trip is the right choice. The rest of the drive is a blast, and it reinforces my ultimate decision to spend the summer away from home, away from my children. There's been no stress in this SUV whatsoever. Carefree chatter is welcomed, and the jokes told are classic. I watch my kids, with their carefree spirits yet remarkable sense of priorities and independence. They've turned out to be amazing adults, on their way to inevitable success.

When we stop for gas mid-trip, Dean and Tina jump out. As soon as they've made their exit, Marsha gives me a nudge. "I think he might have finally found someone as weird as he is," she says.

I'm eyeing them suspiciously. "Yeah, maybe. I guess we'll find out by the end of tomorrow if our dear new Tina's going to make it to a second cut."

"You remember Jackie?" Marsha asks with a teasing cackle.

I drop my forehead into the palm of my hand. Of course, I remember Jackie, she was the single most annoying human I've ever come in contact with. Her laugh was exactly like the hyenas in Disney's *Lion King*, and she spent a large amount of time adjusting the underwire of her bra. How that piece of work honestly made it through three rounds of Dean dates is beyond me.

Dean and Tina jump back into the SUV, putting a quick stop to Marsha and I talking our shit. He willingly handed Tina his keys. She's a much more aggressive driver, taking the turns sharp with a lead foot. In what feels like no time at all we're being navigated by Google Maps to the hotel. Stephany is supposed to be waiting for us in the parking lot to give me the royal tour of her hometown after we've checked in. Marsha and Dean have come here to visit her and spend a week on the beach every summer since they turned sixteen and could drive themselves. They're well acquainted with the area, unlike me, the ol' newbee.

They'd met her at a beachside Bible retreat the year they turned fourteen and formed a pretty solid bond. Stephany is just as strange as they are, so naturally the three of them get along well. I always enjoy her visits and have secretly hoped for years that she's the one Dean would end up with. Sadly, she didn't make it to a second cut because she walked in on him pooping at a Denny's during their date, not paying attention to the men's sign on the bathroom door. He never recovered from the embarrassment, and she couldn't talk to him without laughing for the rest of her stay.

The parking is tight at our charming three-star hotel. After confirming our early check in with Becky at the front desk and acquiring our keys, Dean resumes his rightful place in the driver's seat. He manages to squeeze his SUV in between a shiny new Cadillac and a rusty old pickup. I hear Stephany before I see her. The squeals that she and Marsha let out are piercing and somewhat obnoxious; I love it. I round the vehicle and begin pulling our luggage out from the hatch, and I'm nearly taken to the ground by a hug suitable for a linebacker.

"Carla!" Stephany jumps up and down twice and then grabs my hands. "My parents are so excited that you decided to come out! I think they were getting a little nervous." She pulls her bottom lip down at the edges and squints her eyes, kind of like an 'oh shit' face.

"Yeah, sorry," I admit. "I really haven't given them much time to make other plans." I pull her into another hug. "It's great to see you!"

"You too," she says, returning the second embrace.

We grab our luggage and make our way in. Stephany and Tina seem to hit it off well. Apparently, Stephany has the exact same top hat in her own impressive-sounding dress up stuff. The ironic part is that I'm not surprised in the slightest. Of course, Stephany plays dress up too, I mean, why wouldn't she, right?

We lug all our bags into the elevator, and up to the second floor to find our rooms. Marsha drops herself onto the first bed, letting her arms relax to her sides. Stephany follows suit, and I listen to their meandering and comparing their college classes from the bathroom. I take my time to freshen up my makeup and splay out everything from my bathroom bag across the counter. I continue to eavesdrop. Stephany took the second semester off this year to spend more time with her family before a temporary move to France to finish out her studies in fashion next fall. I'm impressed with her aspirations and look forward to watching her grow a career doing what she loves.

"Mom," Marsha hollers at me. "Are you alive in there?"

I chuckle and dry off my hands. "I'm fine," I half-yell back.

When I come out of the bathroom, the girls haven't moved.

"I'm going downstairs to take a look at the gym before we leave," I tell them. "Want anything from a vending machine?"

"Nope," they say in unison. Marsha sits up and adds, "Do you think it's safe to leave those two weirdos in a room by themselves? I mean, I could always bunk up with Tina tonight and we could make Dean stay in here."

She pulls up her shoulders, and I cut her a dramatic look of panic. "Whatever shall we do?" I say and wave my arms in the air. "Not a grown, drama-loving doctor-to-be, all alone in a double bed hotel room with a girl that we all know he won't have sex with!" I throw my head back and sigh as loud as my nearly emptied lungs will allow.

Little did I know, Dean and Tina were sneaking through the propped open door of our room, on some covert op mission, just in time to hear and see my antics. Marsha and Stephany laugh hysterically, as I turn to see the two of them with their finger guns intact. Their arms raised at the torso, ready to fire if needed, and their faces blank slates - both of them. Tina shows no reaction, nor does Dean. They remain in character of this strange little game of pretend that they're emersed in. A part of me is growing to like her even more because of it. They're definitely two peas in a pod.

Tina leans toward him, as if no one can see or hear what's going on besides them. "Is it against the rules for a lieutenant to have sexual relations with a co-lieutenant?" she whispers before moving her waist around another corner, finger gun first, sweeping the room for danger, no doubt.

Dean drops his own guns in order to lift his hands in aid of a gigantic shrug, "I don't even know if there's such a thing as a *co*-lieutenant."

Dean's grin takes up the larger portion of his face, and he lifts his hands back to a steady shoot out position. His fingers point in the air to match hers. The rest of us watch them, our mouths are slightly agape, because wow. Tina and Dean make a sweep through the room. Their steps are cautious, and there is no space left unchecked. Once they're certain no one is hiding in the closet or beneath any end tables, and that the room is void of 'bugs', they make a grand exit back down the hall and to their own room.

I shake my head. I don't know what to make of what just happened. Neither does Stephany or Marsha. I can tell because they're both sitting up now, staring at the still propped open door, speechless. I clear my throat to snap us all back to reality.

"Yep," I say. "I think they'll be fine."

"Well," Stephany finds her voice. "Glad Dean finally met his match." She falls back to her relaxed position on the bed, staring at the ceiling. "What were you telling me about Professor Stark and your creative writing class?"

Just like that, it's as if Dean and Tina's odd little visit never happened. I turn on my heels, back on track, and find my way to the gym. I prefer to do my working out at night, mornings aren't my thing, so I'm curious to see what this place has to offer me later when I'm ready. I'm actually a little surprised that there's a gym at all. Judging from the uneven trim in the halls and the outdated wallpaper that lines our bathroom walls, this hotel isn't exactly equipped to cater to the luxurious sort. Lucky for me, I prefer to be comfortable in a homey place.

The gym room is small, with only one pulley machine, a few treadmills, one wall lined with mirrors, and a free weight station. I stand and stare for a minute, not at the room in general, but at the one and only person using it. Scratch that, I'm not even staring at him, but at his back... just his back. He's perched on a bench at the free weight station, with his front facing the opposite direction as me.

He's fit, very fit, and I can't seem to find any movement in my own body - my feet are cemented to the floor. My eyes are glued to him. I watch in detail as one drop of sweat works its way from his hairline to the base of his boxers that are peeking out from behind his swim trunks. I watch it roll down the inside of his broad shoulder blade, and across the curve of muscle that lines the outer edge of his spine. Some primal urge inside me wants to walk straight over to him and lick that single drop of salty goodness from his flesh.

Holy shit, Carla, what are you thinking?

My inner voice shouts at me. It's right, too. This man can't be a day over twenty-seven. Can't be. I cut my eyes to the mirrored wall to see the reflection of his young face. The curve of his jaw is sharp, and his icy blues lock onto mine. I don't feel embarrassed, which is even stranger than my random urge to taste his dampened skin. I only stare back, unable to pull away. He smiles a little but holds his steady gaze and continues curling a dumbbell with his left arm. Just as he winks at me, the sound of a cough makes me jump, nearly through the roof.

What the hell just happened? Carla, don't be a cougar, don't be a cougar.

I snap my gaze to the culprit of the cough. It's Tina. She wiggles her eyebrows at me and then gives me the most dramatic wink I've ever seen. Half of her face squinches up with it, as the open-mouthed grin pulls to the side. Then she does a second eyebrow wag for good measure before walking away without saying a word. I watch her hips sway down the hall as her other arm is completely full of probably half of the vending machine goods. She must have beat me down here right after their big protection sweep of my room.

I can feel the color in my cheeks darken a shade, and rather than looking back at the handsome man-boy working out, I turn and stomp away. The last thing I need is to acknowledge the intense moment and let him see the embarrassment seep through the skin on my face. There's no doubt in my mind that he's closer to my kids' age than he is to mine. Which reminds me of Bradley's little fling. Which makes me cringe and shake my head to myself while staring at my open toed sandals while I speed walk away. This of course makes me clip my shoulder against the edge of a corner as I round it. It knocks me somewhat sideways. I rub the pain from it, and grunt at myself in disappointment.

When I get back to the room Marsha and Stephany have already changed into their beachwear and are packing a bag with snacks, water, sunscreen, and the extra hotel towels that we'd requested in advance. Dean is kicked back on one of the beds, also in his swimsuit, waiting for Tina to get ready and join us in my room.

"Wait," I say, "I thought we were going to your house first, Stephany? Now that we've made it here, I'm excited to finally meet your parents and see their condo."

"My mom said to have you there by dinner, and no sooner. Apparently, she's not satisfied with how clean it isn't, and is planning a big meal for everyone."

"Wow, I hope she isn't going out of her way too much. A full summer trip is a lot to prepare for. I don't want to take away from all the other stuff she surely has to do. We could even pick up a pizza or something on our way?" I suggest.

"Nope," Stephany argues, with no intention of calling her mom to try and change her mind. "They're all packed and ready. My mom is a planner and a neat freak. You'll see. Dinner will be nice, the condo will be spotless, and you haven't put her out at all. The very second I got off the phone with Marsha last night she sat down with a pen and paper to make herself a shopping list for dinner, and a checklist of everything to have accomplished before you arrived."

I lean against the wall and fold my arms over my

chest, feeling a little guilty for being so much trouble. "Sounds thorough," I say.

Marsha pokes her head out of the bathroom. "Don't feel bad, mom," she encourages. "You're doing them a favor. Plus, you're going to love Sarah! She enjoys hosting dinners and is thrilled that you finally decided to come out and see the condo before they leave town."

"It's true," Stephany agrees. "Being thorough is kind of her thing. She's weird like that."

"Okaaaay," I say hesitantly before relaxing my arms to my sides, letting out a huff of air and reaching for my bag. "So, the beach then?"

It isn't very far to drive. In fact, we could have walked, and a part of me wishes we would have. It's a charming little city and I'm dying to check out the antique shop that we passed between the hotel and the beach. There must be some amazing old books there. We wrestle a few fold-up beach chairs out of the back hatch and find the perfect spot. The sun is out, but there's a slight breeze which makes the temperature perfect to soak up a few rays. I lather on a thick layer of sunscreen and don one of the floppy sun hats that Marsha had picked out of Tina's prop bag. It reminds me of the little girl in my dream, which gives me mixed feelings; but I wear it anyway.

After a good hour of alternating sides and taking the occasional stroll to the water's edge to cool my feet while watching my adult children and their friends splash around like fools, I decide to take a walk. I let them know the direction I'm headed and that I won't be long. Each of my steps squish into the sand, leaving dissolvable, wet-looking footprints behind my bare feet. My sandals dangle from my fingertips. There are a few dozen people littering the beach around us, everyone spaced out and enjoying the waves. I smile at a couple of kids as they build a castle and giggle at each other's jokes. Maybe it won't be so lonely here, after all.

Glancing down the shoreline I spot a familiar man. Correction, a familiar man-boy's back and swim trunks. He's running toward a beautiful young girl in a sun-gold bikini, the same girl who checked us in at the hotel, and my stomach sinks at the sight of them. I freeze in my tracks and look frantically in all directions for something I can hide behind. There's a huge shade umbrella only a few paces away, so I make a run for it. I don't know why I feel like I need to hide from him. Maybe it's because of my embarrassment of Tina's silent tease, or because I don't know if my nervous chest can handle another intense stare down and adorable wink. All I know is that my body seems to have an electrical pulse that's pulling me to him like a tractor beam, and all I want to do is disappear into the background.

Luckily, the owners of this shade umbrella seem to be missing. I kneel behind it, careful not to wrinkle my favorite lacey white swim dress, as it covers the navy one piece hugging my small curves. I should go back to my spot, to my kids. I know that if I turn now, he'll never see me. Never recognize me from behind. He doesn't know me, and I don't know him. Our moment wasn't even a moment, just my drooling all over myself like a kid in a candy shop. Why am I obsessing, and why haven't I gone back to my rightful spot yet?

Rather than turning and standing with my face and body opposite his direction, like I know I should, I peek my head slowly around the umbrella. Just one look won't hurt, I convince myself. I watch as the man-boy finishes his charge at the girl. He scoops her over his shoulder and races into the waves, packing her like Bradley used to our children when they were little. He called it a sack of potatoes and it made them laugh so hard that once Marsha even peed on him. Right down his shoulder and chest. As much as I want to laugh at the memory, I can't. I'm too introverted into myself as I watch the water work its way through this guy's swim bottoms. I can't believe I'm actually hiding and spying on a man-boy. *Who are you, Carla?*

A small child squeals next to me. I look over to see her pointing at me, "Daddy, Daddy, I think we're being robbed!" She shouts with her accusatory finger a few inches from my face.

"No, no, I, I..." I stand and fidget with the hem of my dress. "Sorry, I just." I'm trying to keep my back to the man-boy as the father to this little squealer stares at me with his eyebrows lifted almost to his hairline and an amused grin on his face. Clearly, he thinks my discomfort and stutter is funny. "Sorry." I finally say and let out a sigh. "I wasn't stealing, I promise. I just tripped."

For the second time today, my cheeks are flushed. The child's humorous father dismisses me with a friendly wave, and I storm off, back toward my family so that I can wallow in my embarrassment in peace. I refuse to look back over toward the water line and can only pray that I wasn't spotted spying. Not sure if I can admit to myself, let alone a complete stranger, that I've allowed myself to daydream of him yet again today.

The rest of the time on the beach is spent sipping

lemonade and being lost in my thoughts. For a moment, I consider the possibility of turning back for home and tossing this entire summer vacation to the wind. What if the man-boy did see me watching him again? What if he lives here, is only dating the girl from the hotel rather than staying there, and I see him all the time over the summer? But then again, he clearly has a girlfriend, so it shouldn't matter if I ever run into him. One that he's comfortable enough with to toss over his muscular shoulders like a rag doll. I wonder what it would feel like - to be tossed around like that - and in other ways. I can't weigh any more than that little tart, and he didn't even hesitate or struggle. I wonder what other parts of him don't hesitate or struggle? The thought makes me flush, again, and I take another sip of my drink.

"Mom!" Marsha intrudes on my sweaty thoughts as she plops herself down into her chair next to mine. "What's the deal? You've been staring into space for like twenty minutes. I don't think you've even blinked." She reaches into the cooler and pulls out a bottle of water to sip on. "You were weird this morning, too." She points out.

"Yeah well," I sigh, "I guess I'm just trying to figure out what's going on with my life. I'm getting old, Marsha."

"Nope."

"Yes I am."

"No, I said nope because that isn't it. Spit it out, Mom, what's weighing so heavily on your mind? Don't lie either, I'll know."

"Ugh," I groan. She's right, of course, so before I can even give it a second thought, I blurt, "Are you pregnant?"

Marsha spits her water all down the front of herself and then sits up, nearly doubling over in her seat with laughter. "What!?" she shouts, wholly amused at my question.

I explain the dream, and my lingering accusations of them wanting to get rid of me. As I say the words out loud, I realize just how silly it all sounds. I leave out everything about the guy I'd been caught watching twice today. Marsha doesn't need to know anything about that huge embarrassment.

She assures me that I have nothing to worry about in terms of becoming a grandma any time soon. She's even agreeable that it could easily be years down the line that I'm dreaming about, and more than anything else, she's excited about my dream. "Now we know that at least one of us is destined to procreate, right?" she says, bringing us both a strange sort of ease.

I relax into my chair and push away all thoughts other than those of my family, and my blessings. Marsha is right, I have nothing to be worried about. Even the unnerving daydreams of the young guy with a gorgeous girl and sexy back are brushed aside. I think I'll give the summer on the beach a chance after all.

CHAPTER 4

I DO LOVE Sarah, and I love the condo even
more. Meeting Stephany's parents is a delight, and the full medley of Italian dishes she's pre-
pared is divine. As Italy is where they'll be spending
the summer, she thought it appropriate to serve lin-
guini with clam sauce, freshly baked bread on the
side, and *nocciolini di canzo* for dessert.

When our dinner is finished, I inform them that
I've made up my mind and will be accepting their
offer to house-sit for the summer. I let them know that
I should be able to come back in less than two weeks
to stay for the long haul.

"Perfect timing," Sarah announces with a
gleaming hop. "We'll be catching out flight in just a
couple days. We can always have a neighbor water
the plants if it takes you any longer than make it back.
Otherwise, that would work out just right!"

My twins are only slightly surprised to hear that
the paperwork for an extended leave from the bank
had already been started, the dirty schemers. Sarah
and her husband are relieved to hear the reassurance

that they wouldn't have to scramble to find someone else last minute.

Together, the two of them give me a full tour of their home, welcoming me in with open arms. I'll be staying in the guest room, and although it's a spare, it's even more spacious and friendly than the master bedroom in my own home. It has a walk-in closet, its own bathroom, and even a reading nook, cozied into a bay window that reaches the full height of the vaulted ceiling. It's picture perfect, making my own bedside reading bench seem nothing more than cute in comparison. The colors are a complimenting pink, teal, and ivory. A perfect fit for the walkout patio that overlooks the ocean. The condo is beautiful, but I think it's safe to say that my own summer bedroom is the best spot of the entire home.

They leave me alone to make myself comfortable in my new space while they work together to clean up dinner. I offer to help, but Sarah won't even hear it. Insisting that until they leave, I'm a guest and will be treated as such. I walk out onto my own private patio, stretch my arms into the air and glance down the row of beachside condos that are in line with this one. They're all just as gorgeous with lots of space between each to offer plenty of privacy and comfort. I strain my eyes into the horizon. It's faint, but from here I can catch a glimpse of the stunning peer that stretches impressively into the water, darting out from the center of the city. The view is breathtaking, and I'm starting to get the feeling that once the summer is over, I won't want to go back home. I already don't.

After a comfortable chat to accompany a couple glasses of wine with Stephany and her parents, the kids and I retreat to the hotel. Marsha and I both sleep like babies and judging by the energy protruding from Dean and Tina the next morning, they did too. We pack up our bags and hit the road just as check-out time chimes.

Monday proves to be blissful, as I hand Mark my papers first thing in the morning and he passes along the news of its approval by the end of the workday. HR didn't mess around or waste any time in my case. I suppose Mark's conversation with Danika really did go exactly as he said it would. He let me know that her meeting with the board went well, and they were all in a prompt agreement to this being my final pre-leave week, before returning at the end of the summer.

Having such a soul-warming trip to the condo and being approved for my leave so quick and seamlessly, kind of makes the rest of the week drag on. My bags are packed by Wednesday, aside from the toiletries that I need to use throughout the remainder of the week. Marsha and Dean both ace the bulk of their tests, leaving only a few more to take before the school year comes to a close. We celebrate the week's success and my summer-to-be on Friday night, and I don't waste any time hitting the road. I foresaw myself being a little bit more hesitant to take off, maybe even staying home for a few days without work, but I found myself getting antsy. By Sunday morning I'm telling the twins my goodbyes and blowing a heartfelt kiss to them out my car window before watching my house shrink in the rearview.

I drive straight to the condo in Cayucos, no pit stops, no potty breaks, no meandering around anywhere between. The garage door opener that Sarah had given me is clipped to my sun visor, making the press of its button feel like home. The door lifts smoothly and silently, much different from the clanking of my own as it struggles to make the round each time. I sigh and close it behind myself. The mud room entrance from the garage leads directly into the kitchen where I set my purse down on the thick slab of granite covering the middle island, next to an un-opened bottle of Moscato and a note addressed to me.

Carla,

We're thrilled that you decided to stay in our home for the summer! I usually water the plants three times a week and there are plenty of cleaning supplies to last the duration of your stay in the mud room. I didn't leave much food, as I assume you have your own pref-erences. We usually box up most everything in the fridge the day before we leave and donate it to the local food drive for children in need. There's a hide-a-key inside the hanging azalea plant on the front porch, just in case there's ever an issue with the garage or your spare set. Help yourself to anything and everything. Our home is yours. Or, as they say in Italy, la mia casa e ta tua casa! Please let us know when you've arrived. Have a wonderful summer!

-Sarah and Timothy

MY GOD, THEY'RE nice, I think. I pick up my phone and send Sarah a quick text, letting her know I've made it, as well as thanking her again for everything.

Then I slip off my shoes and mosey through my new summer living space, quietly absorbing every room in all its serenity and grace. They'd given me a tour just over a week ago, but this feels different. I run my fingertips softly across the lacey throw-over that's draped on the back of a cozy sectional in the living room, before stopping at the entrance of Timothy's study.

The door is open, inviting me in, and although crossing the threshold feels a little strange as one man's office is never a place for peering eyes, he'd urged me during my tour to help myself to his bookshelves. I hadn't actually gone inside this room last weekend, but now that I'm here to stay, I can't help but let my curiosity and love of books keep me away. At a snail's pace, I step inside and an involuntary gasp escapes my lips. What Timothy had played off as a few humble shelves of both hard, and paperbacks is nothing short of an in-home library fit for royalty. Each wall is lined from ceiling to floor, and the room is rounded, making the slide ladder glide a full room's loop with ease. His desk is mahogany, fairly small, and in addition there's a standalone printer, and two plush, extra cozy looking armchairs to read in. The entire office seems to be built to hold only books.

What makes this in-home library even better, if that's possible at all, is that it isn't categorized by genre or title and author, but by color. Compliments of Sarah no doubt. I'm beginning to realize just how impressive this couple really is. No wonder Stephany is always such a delight. I close my eyes tightly and stretch my neck from side to side, before dropping it backwards and spinning myself in a small circle. I don't even know where to start, so I decide that a short game of Spin-the-Carla will point me toward an amusing section of color.

I stop, plant my feet after jumping up and down a couple times and shaking my hands to my sides for luck, and then open my eyes. "All shades violet it is," I tell myself as it's the first color I see. I glance through the titles on the shelf that first pulled my attention, and after skipping over a few thriller and fantasy novels, I settle on a critically acclaimed, *The Color Purple* by Alice Walker. Why not something so historically rich and compelling to bury myself in on the first few nights of my stay?

The rest of the condo is just as gorgeous as I remember it being. I unload my bags, filling the closet, bathroom, and empty dresser with my things. I'd packed pretty much every item of clothing I own, although now I'm thinking that the sweaters and hoodies may have been a bit of an overkill. It takes me hours to arrange my stuff and to water all of the plants. The condo has only been completely empty for a couple of days now, so it's perfect timing to keep them hydrated and healthy. I smile to myself, affirming the choice to come sooner than later before grabbing my keys and heading for the door.

An adorable grocery store, owned by locals rather than a chain, is a mere five-minute drive from the condo. I walk through the aisles slowly, familiarizing myself with it as I fill my cart to the brim. I'm not a big fan of eating out, aside from pizza night, but now that I'm so far away from the delivery guy that I adore seeing so often, I have no intention of keeping up such an unhealthy routine.

The young girl at the checkout counter is friendly,

she smiles at me with her full red lips. "Thanks for shopping here, Ma'am," she says in a kind gesture.

By the time I get back, put everything away and scarf down a sub sandwich, the sun is beginning to dip into the horizon. So, I slip on something a little more comfortable, grab my book and step out of my room onto the patio overlooking the waves. The lighting that comes out from the opened curtains of the bay window is the perfect amount to see the pages clearly, yet I'm comfortably concealed in the darkening evening from any possible onlookers in the line of other condos along the beachside.

I'm instantly sucked into the story and before I know it the sun has completely disappeared, and the stars now shine as far as I can see. Practically all of the neighbor's lights have gone out, except for one, and I can hear a very faint voice coming from beneath it. I can see the silhouette of a man and hear in his raised voice that he's yelling angrily, but I can't quite make out what he's saying. It's three condos down, and I can't help but to wonder what he's so mad about. Which isn't like me at all. I'm hardly ever nosey - to each their own. However, this is going to be my home for the next three months. If there's a man with a raunchy temper or terrible nighttime habits, then I might want to know about it. Prepare myself to avoid any kind of a run in, if need be.

I'd seen a pair of binoculars on one of the shelves in Timothy's den, so I go inside, fetch them as quickly as possible, and hurry back out, hoping that I haven't missed anything from the ranting man down the way. I sit back in my seat, crossing my fingers and my toes that I can get a good look at the guy's face.

My heart sinks to the bottom of my chest as I witness him hold the phone that he's yelling into away from his ear to scream an audible "Eat shit!" into the receiver before tossing it onto a chair. He picks up a bottle of rum, chugs the last few swallows remaining in the bottom of it, and then throws the empty bottle as hard as he can against the concrete. It shatters, and I gasp, the blood pumping through my veins speeding up a notch. I pull the binoculars away from my face and hold my hand on my chest to steady the pounding inside of it a little.

"Oh my God," I whisper, before taking another look.

The second I place the circular glass ends back up against the skin around my eyes, my heart stops beating completely, for only a second though before slamming back to start like a kickdrum. He's looking right at me, and it's the man-boy from the hotel and the beach last weekend. His eyes are glassed over, his face sagging in my direction in his drunkenness, and his chest rises and falls in shallow breath. I'm busted, and he's a maniac, a temper tantrum throwing menace. A handsome angry man that has totally caught me watching him, yet again, this time much less pleasant than the first. My first thoughts are of those rippling muscles and the way he'd carelessly thrown the girl on the beach over his shoulder with such ease. If he were to come at me for spying, I wouldn't stand a chance.

Naturally, I panic and run, my bare feet padding through the condo in a speedy race to double check that every single door and window is locked. I grab my phone and type out a text to Sarah asking if there are any psychopaths on the loose in her neighborhood, but then I delete it. The last thing I want to do is alarm them on the first night of my stay, or to make them second guess their choice of a house sitter. Especially after we've been phone friends, keeping tabs on each other's children for so many years. I call each of my kids, and they don't answer. So, I type out a second message. It's to both of them, in a group text, telling them to check in with me tomorrow morning, first thing, and if I don't answer then it's because I've been killed by Stephany's psychotic neighbor three condos down.

I lean my back against the front door and catch my breath. What the hell am I supposed to do now? I won't be able to sleep, or even to read, now that my heart is racing, and my mind is on a reel. Plus, I left my book outside on the chair. What the hell was I thinking, to spy on my new neighbor anyway? Of course, I was bound to get busted in the act, and it just had to be that particular man-boy too. The sexy guy that I shouldn't have ever noticed in the first place has likely now put me on some sort of a hit list.

"Stop it, Carla," I tell myself before stomping to the kitchen to make a cup of tea and search for a comfort snack. Maybe a hot drink, something with chamomile, and some food will calm me down.

With nervous, slightly shaky fingers I prepare a small plate of cheese, crackers and pepperoni while my tea steeps in the water. Then I take my goods and retreat to the couch, rather than my room with its door so close to where I was caught spying. I debate pushing something heavy in front of the bedroom door, just in case of a break-in, but talk myself out of it. If anything terrible really were to happen, at least I've given my children a heads up on who the detectives should question. Not only that, but the rest of the other people between me and him must have heard him yelling as well. It would take a fool to seek out any sort of wrongdoing after such a boisterous outburst, surely the whole shoreline was awakened by his tantrum, right?

"Carla," I tell myself as I scroll through a few mindless reality television shows, "You have nothing to worry about."

Finally, I settle for a nature channel, something far from scary or suggestive. I watch until my food and tea are gone, and over time I fall asleep. As I wake in the morning the sun is shining into all of the east-facing windows, its golden light pouring over the house plants. It's beautiful, and although I didn't sleep in the room that I was previously so excited to stay in, I still feel refreshed. I try my darndest to push away thoughts of the neighbor down the way, with his foul language and horrible temper.

Choosing something for breakfast is a little hard, and it makes me miss having Marsha around to cook. The weight of a brick suddenly rests in my stomach, making me wonder if this is what it feels like to be homesick. I wind up settling for a mere piece of toast and black coffee, before vowing to make this summer worth the time away. I reach for the notepad that Sarah had left my welcome note on, rip off that top page and set to making a checklist of a few things to work toward during my time here.

The list includes a variety of genres that I want to read, a certain amount of workout routines I want accomplished such as how many pushups, squats and sit ups in one go by the end of summer. Which reminds me to find and enroll myself in a gym. I also challenge myself to make a few friends, go on at least three social gatherings of sorts, and to spend at least one day per week on the beach -- be it directly outside the condo or at the public area--whether I feel like it or not. Once I'm satisfied with my list, I turn on some uplifting music to blare through my new bedroom - a room that I'll be sleeping in from now on, period. I jump in the shower, ready to charge the summer ahead.

Now that I've been living in this glorious condo for a couple of weeks, it's time to meet my neighbors. I've purchased a couple of treat baskets that I intend on taking to the neighbors directly on each side of me, clearly not the one three doors down, but have yet to deliver. I've grown to quite like the serenity and the peace and quiet. I've even finished a couple of books from Timothy's library, saving the antique shopping for when I run out of comfort in my solitude. I still have two and a half months of my three months left, and the lack of a checkmark by the making friends line on my list isn't going anywhere. This condo is amazing, and thus far I've chosen to spend my committed beach time at the local bay, avoiding the back patio and private seaside view all together. It's calling to me though, and I may have to brave the notion of spending more time just out my own back door. I can't avoid the summer menace down the way much longer; it'll ruin my entire stay.

When I finally decide to deliver my neighborly gifts and introduce myself, I nearly trip on an object that's been placed on the front porch. It catches my toe with a pointy spike, making me cuss, gasp for a breath and nearly drop my baskets. It didn't hurt, but it scared the shit out of me. I look around my armful of goods to see a pineapple, wobbling around after its disturbance, and there's a card sitting beneath it. I set the baskets down on one of the decorative wicker chairs on the porch and reach down to pick up the fruit and card. I rip open the top and pull out a recipe card. It's for a hollowed-out pineapple and rum punch. *Sounds amazing.* I make a mental note to go straight to the liquor store after delivering my baskets. I flip over the recipe card to find a handwritten note on the back.

It's addressed to me but doesn't say my name. It says:

To the beautiful woman looking after this condo,

Sorry for the disturbance a while back, I think we got off on the wrong foot. Based on your dress the first time I saw you, I have a feeling you like pineapples. If you need anything at all, you know where I live.

Yours, Blake

I READ IT about five times over. Blake, Blake, Blake. I think of his face, the distinct jawline and sharp icy blues, the name fits. The tips of my fingers begin to get a little numb, and I can feel my cheeks heat up as I recall the crazed look on his face after he'd shattered a bottle and caught me spying on him... with binoculars no less. He totally just acknowledged it too. He knows that I know where he lives. He isn't mad about my spying either, he got me a gift. Unless it's a trap. *Oh my God, what if it's a trap?* I shake the crazy from my mind. It can't be. We all have bad days. Even with as unsettled as I felt that night, and with the strange aching in my knees right now as I read the small yet impactful note over and over and over again, I manage to talk myself into seeing the good.

I think of all the drunken phone conversations I had with Bradley during our divorce. I'm pretty sure I even screamed those exact words into the phone before. I've never downed an entire bottle of rum and then slammed it against the cement, but that's not to say Bradley never did. I draw in a calming breath, set the pineapple and note in the second wicker chair and get back to my business at hand. I have baskets to deliver, and friends to make, why the hell am I obsessing over this handsome young stranger, yet again? I'll tend to the liquor store and make myself this drink later.

I deliver both baskets and introduce myself. To the right of me is an elderly couple, very friendly, but I could smell the stench of cat pee the very second the woman opened the door. In the two weeks of my stay so far, I've yet to see a cat, so they must keep them inside always. As soon as the door swings open, I gag and have to play it off like I'm feeling under the weather. I decline her offer to come inside for tea. She calls her husband from across the room to greet me at the door. It takes him a good three minutes to make his way there using a walker. He is kind, and sincere, and I feel kind of bad about not taking them up on a cup of tea. Sadly, I'm not too confident in my ability to ignore the smell of their home. I see at least five different cats passing the entrance, and when they invite me a second time, I say no again and turn away as kindly as possible. I don't mind cats, but the smell of too many, is well, too much. I think I can safely check these neighbors off of the possible friend list.

The couple to the right of me seems to be a bit more up to my speed. It's the husband who answers the door. His smile is genuine and friendly, and the way he has their sleeping baby draped over his fairly narrow shoulder tells me practically everything I need to know.

"Tyler," he says, extending a free hand for me to shake before relieving me of the basket.

This time I accept the invitation inside but insist that I can only stay a few minutes. I don't want to press my welcome. No sooner than he hollers a kind "Jacklyn," up the stairs, I'm nearly taken out by a wizzz of a speeding toddler in a wheeled baby-walker. The little one maneuvering it has short red pigtails, a giggle that instantly warms my heart, and a pink sippy cup of juice in her hand.

"Don't mind that one," Tyler says with an upbeat chuckle. "She practically lives in that thing. She can almost walk on her own, but we just can't bring ourselves to get rid of it yet. Keeps her contained while we manage the twins."

"Wait, twins?" I ask, the joy in my center building. Just as I open my mouth to tell him of my own twins, Jacklyn graces us with her presence. She walks carefully down the steps as the baby in her arms is concealed by a breastfeeding cover. It's tucked neatly around her on every side, keeping herself and the baby concealed, and her unoccupied arm is out ready to shake my hand. It's a firm, confident gesture much like her husband's.

"Jacklyn," she says with a smile. "You must be Carla! Sorry we haven't made it over to introduce ourselves. Sarah told me all about you, she just adores your children. You have twins the same age as Stephany, right?"

I'm surprised at how instantly comfortable I am around Jacklyn and Tyler. I'm drawn into their family charm. "I do! They just turned twenty last fall, but I can remember answering the door with one sleeping while the other one used *me* like I was his binky, like it was yesterday."

"You too, huh?" She rolls her eyes but follows it with a light smirk. "It's easier to let him stay attached all the time than to listen to him cry all day."

"I know the feeling exactly. My Dean was the same. Although, if he knew I just told you that he'd be gunnin' for me." We laugh it off, but little do they know, the last time I embarrassed him over something harmless and silly, he happily returned the favor. He played practical jokes on me for a week. He and Marsha got quite the kick out of putting flour in my blow dryer especially.

They talk me into sitting down in the kitchen and joining them for a quick glass of wine. The banter between the two is comfortable. The toddler, who's name I learn is Lola, circles us around the table and crashes into the wall a few times. She also talks a lot of gibberish, somewhat sing-song style, and she likes to throw her sippy cup against the kitchen cupboards. She's aiming for the sink. Apparently Tyler made a game of it, hoping that eventually she'd make it in, which meant cleaning up after herself, but it really only slams the cupboard below, splashing juice from its rim all over the place. Before I know it, my quick glass of wine has turned into a full hour of getting to know my rambunctious temporary neighbors.

Tyler is a networking engineer. He gets paid a salary, and only spends a few hours a week at work. Most of his stuff can be done remotely from home. This comes in handy as their twins are only four months old and Jacklyn spends the majority of her time with the chubbier boy, Hoss, attached to the boob. This leaves Jaxx, the less demanding of the two, needing little more than Tyler's shoulder for draping himself over to sleep.

"It's his favorite spot," Tyler giggles, and turns to the side so I can see the little one's face all squished up and resting on his tiny arms, just at the base of Tyler's hairline. "It actually works out okay. I've learned to bend at the knees anytime I need to pick anything up. My balance is improving by the day."

Tyler's even made a makeshift sling of sorts to help hold the baby in place. What once was a mommy wrap, meant to hold the newborn gently against a parent's chest, is now a shoulder drape. It's wrapped from one side of Tyler's neck, over the baby, and tucked carefully under his opposite armpit.

Jacklyn, for only thirty-two years old, has quite the success story of her own. She passed the bar at twenty-five and landed a job in a very prestigious firm in Seattle. The two met when his previous company was contracted to do some work on the computer systems at her firm. After two moves together, a beachside elopement, and running her own small family practice she decided on a temporary leave so that they could start a family together before she got any older. The very month she quit taking her birth control they were pregnant with Lola, and life still hasn't slowed for the adorable little family in the making.

"So, you've been here for two weeks already?"

Jacklyn asks. "We spend quite a bit of time out back on the beach, why haven't we seen you out there?"

"Yeah," Tyler adds, "I remember when we first moved here. We practically lived out back. Our beach is beautiful. There's even a family of dolphins who stick around close. We haven't had a shark scare, like, ever."

What do I say? I have a weird, inexplicable secret crush on the guy who lives a couple condos away, one that's closer to their age than mine, and who likely has the dangerous temper of a menace well-worth avoiding? Even just considering the fact in mind, I realize how dumb my reasoning for avoiding my own back yard is. I also realize that picturing the boxer line under *his* swim trunks, and even his angry tantrum is making me kind of wet between the legs. *Blake, tell them Blake is the reason you've avoided the most beautiful part of your summer condo, Carla you wimp.* I know exactly how gorgeous and perfect the beach really is, so my excuse is no excuse at all. I drum my fingernails nervously on the tabletop, and down the remainder of my drink in one filling gulp.

"Sorry," I can feel the skin of my cheeks darken as I lie, "I guess I've been shy. I went to the public area by the peer a couple times, it's easier to hide in large groups. Spending beach time just outside the condo feels too surreal in a way."

My fingers continue to drum.

Jacklyn and Tyler glance at each other, their looks of speculation mirroring one another perfectly. They can obviously see through my bullshit, but lucky for me they don't call me on it. Jacklyn's eyes open wide and a full grin pulls her face upward. She even bounces on her seat a little in excitement which causes little Hoss to belt out a squeal of disapproval from beneath her cover. She reaches under to adjust him, likely sliding her human pacifier back in his mouth, and after a little shoulder cringe as he latches, she finally reveals the reasoning behind her sudden happy thoughts.

"You should join us this Friday!" she says. "We're having a barbeque outback! A few friends are coming, nothing too big. We had one last year to bring in the summer, and it was a big hit. So much fun! My parents will be coming for a visit to keep the kids inside and put to bed properly, so that we can relax and let loose a little."

"Oh, I couldn't possibly impose," I begin and put my hands in the air, as if I'm gearing up to defend myself for some reason.

"Nonsense!" Tyler almost shouts, causing Jacklyn and I both to jump and her to giggle in response. The sleeping baby on his shoulder doesn't budge. "Jacklyn hasn't had a drink since before she was pregnant. It's exactly what we both need, and you're definitely invited. Our friends are welcoming, you'll have a great time."

I shake my head a little, but before I can say another word they say in unison, "We insist!"

"Well, I think my kids will be coming out for a visit. I planned on going home for the weekend to see them, but they're insisting on coming here. Maybe we'll swing by, but only for a little while, I really don't want to press my welcome."

And with that, almost like a warning siren, little Jaxx begins to wiggle and squirm before bawling out a scream suitable for a toddler, rather than a newborn. This child really has a healthy set of pipes on him. I use his begging scream for a change as my cue to leave, and after having thanked them for the drink and their warm hospitality I bid farewell and break for the door. I speed walk down the sidewalk, up my walkway, then I grab my pineapple and note on my way to the door without so much as looking down the road. I don't want to know if Blake is out, and I don't want to be caught looking in his direction again either... ever.

This little gathering on Friday will happen whether I make up some excuse to get out of it or not. The wine they'd fed me was delicious and has me feeling a little tipsy, so naturally I'm questioning every one of my thoughts since finding the damn pineapple. There will be no reading on the patio yet again tonight. Even just a note from this Blake human has me on edge, especially as I'm holding it.

Less than two hours ago, I'd convinced myself that he's normal and nice. Now, the possibility of him gracing a random social event with his presence has the blood in my veins lit ablaze. Tyler and Jacklyn didn't even mention it being a neighborhood party; they said friends. Maybe I should have asked? But then, how would that have looked? Wow, I'm really losing it, and for what? No, for who? I don't even know him, but I'm obsessed. Maybe I'm just bored, and there's no one else around to obsess over.

I'm grateful to have made friends, especially such laid-back ones... and with twins, how exciting is that? I'd be a fool not to attend their party. But, what if he's there?

I groan, drop myself into a heap on the couch and throw my head back. "Damnnit Carla, what's wrong with you?!"

<h1 style="text-align:center">CHAPTER 5</h1>

FRIDAY MORNING ROLLS around quicker than I'd have liked it to. I'm a nervous wreck, and after a vicious game of mental Ping-Pong, back and forth for days, trying to decide whether or not to go to this silly barbeque, I've made up my mind. I'm going. I'm taking my kids for support, even though they know nothing about Blake, the pineapple-gifting anxiety maker. It'll help to have them there. I've marked off making friends on my list, as Jacklyn has even stopped by here since my introduction to bring a treat basket of my own to return the favor.

She stayed for a couple of hours, until Tyler called for help with all three kids screaming at him in the background. It was a second nice visit, and she's an amazing baker. All the more reason to go through with the party. I'm sure talking my kids into going will be no trouble at all. The mention of a beachside bar-beque, practically in the backyard, will surely give them both reason to celebrate the very second they walk through the door, which should have been by now, come to think of it.

I wonder what's holding them up? Hopefully it

isn't Tina. I liked her, but I also want to delay any possibility of my dream coming true any time soon. The little girl who called me C'ma has yet to make a second sleepful appearance, and as much as I'd love to have another little one in my life someday... that day isn't now.

It's late afternoon, my kids should be here any minute. The party is in a couple of hours, and I'm still in my pajamas. I finished off a Hoover novel today which nearly sucked the life out of me, I ugly cried and everything. Great book but a bad choice for this day, because it's made me even more nervous about Blake showing up to the damn barbeque. It's exactly the kind of thing that would happen in one of Colleen's stories, and now paranoia has crawled under my skin to accompany anxiety. That book and Blake may as well be holding hands and skipping down the road, whistling heart attack, each with a pineapple drink in hand.

I spread a few summer dresses across my bed and stare at them disapprovingly. Too frilly, too cutesy, too young, or too plain, each and every choice is a fail. "Ugh," I groan and shake my head. *I should have gone shopping*, I think, but then again, I don't want to seem desperate. Or feel desperate, either. I tap my foot on the plush carpet before texting Marsha that the front door is unlocked, and then stomping angrily to the shower.

The soap bubbles fresh rose scented, and no sooner than I'm out and smoothing a thick layer of shimmering body butter with a smell to match over my flesh, I hear Dean and Marsha arguing over the television remote. I smile. Listening to the sound of their voices from down the hall, rather than on the other end of a phone receiver, makes me feel more at home than I have since I got here. The hair dryer and curling irons work their magic almost as thoroughly as my makeup does. I secure a towel around myself, walk into my room and stare at the dresses again. Still, the same disappointment consumes me.

I opt for my sexiest black lace panties and bra to make me feel naughty beneath, and cover them up with a simple, yet flattering floral tank top and a pair of jeans that hugs my curves tightly. The best of both worlds. I get to feel naughty yet comfortable all at once, now all I need to do is settle for a nice open toe wedge shoe, and I'm all set.

"Mom!" Marsha shouts, as I walk down the hall. "Wow, look at you. Going on a date?"

Crap, I drop my chin to my chest. I was going for simple, not subtle. I raise my hands to my sides and stare down at my outfit. "What are you talking about, I'm wearing jeans."

"Noooo," Dean chimes in, "you're wearing date worthy jeans and you have extra make-up on."

I blow a lungful of air through my nearly closed lips causing them to rumble, like a horse, and I plop myself down on the couch between the two of them. It doesn't feel like two weeks since I saw them in person at all. It feels like we've picked right back up on some random conversation we'd already been having for days on end. This very moment reminds me of when they were in their mid-teens and they'd stay with their dad for a week or two at a time. I'd miss them so badly that my bones would ache, but then when they returned home it felt like they'd never left. They're every bit as much a part of me as my own flesh and bone, like a limb -- or two. Marsha, my right leg, and Dean my left.

"How do you guys feel about going to a barbeque on the beach tonight?" I ask.

Marsha sits up straight and bounces slightly on her tush, "I knew it. You met someone already, didn't you? It's like a date!"

Dean rolls his eyes at her tenacity before throwing me a side nod. "Who's the lucky guy?" He wonders.

"No one!" I scold them. "It's been just under three weeks, my hell. No lucky guy. No date. Just a nice pair of jeans and a little extra makeup so that I can take my grown ass children with me to dinner at the neighbors'!"

Dean leans forward to look around me completely, and locks eyes with Marsha. They stare each other down. The moment's intense. Their eyes are wide and occasionally one wiggles their nose, and the other gives a light nod. I clear my throat, knowing exactly where this is going. Dean leans back, resumes the exact same position that he was previously in with his attention glued to a shark show, and then they both blurt in unison. "Who's the guy?"

My mind automatically pictures Blake, and not even the handsome chiseled body and his reflection in the mirror winking at me either. Rather, the impulse of my thoughts goes to his angry, drunken-rage face. The Blake that had just shattered glass on his own patio before looking up to find me spying on him. An angry swarm of bees fills my belly, and I hold my breath. I can feel my nostrils flare and in my right side peripheral I can see the entertained light shining through Marsha's eyes.

"I'm not having this conversation," I say, and

jump to my feet. I stomp off to the kitchen and shout at them while opening the fridge to stress eat, "How was the drive, anyway? I thought you'd be here hours ago."

Marsha follows me in and drops herself onto a barstool. Dean remains glued to the show, ready to join in the conversation only if he feels like it.

"Dean was going to bring some chick."

"Sarah," he shouts over his shoulder.

"But, after we waited on her for half the day, he finally caved into my impatience and we left her behind."

"Makes sense," I say.

Dean shouts again, "What exactly makes sense? It isn't like she stood me up."

Marsha shouts back at him, "Just because she texted you every twenty minutes begging you to wait, doesn't mean she actually wanted to come. She was testing you to see how long you'd actually wait for her. Giving you a taste of your own medicine."

"Whatever," he says with a shrug. He doesn't seem too heartbroken, so I leave it as is.

Marsha keeps at it. "You probably broke the heart of some friend of hers, so she was playing you all morning. Wasting my time in the process."

To that he says nothing, only turns up the volume to the television.

"What about Tina?" I ask neither of them in particular. "I kind of liked that one."

Marsha does the talking, as Dean is now deaf to anything other than whatever knowledge about great whites is blaring through the front room speakers. "They went out two more times, and she thought she owned him. Needy..."

"Well, that's too bad," I shrug.

I recall my dream and consider asking if they'd ever fooled around, but I instantly think better of it.

Marsha convinces me that the store-bought cheesecake I'd planned on taking to Jacklyn and Tyler's barbeque is a less-than-worthy dish. Apparently, she wouldn't be caught dead showing up to a social event full of people she's never met with this less-than-mediocre contribution. I should have known. I suppose this means we'll be eating cheesecake for the remainder of the weekend, and therefore I'll need to add another twenty minutes to my gym time for the next several days to make up for it. The extra work I've been putting in is already paying off. I can even see a small line forming from my ribcage to panty-line. I haven't had that in over a decade, so I'll be damned if I let a cheesecake weekend ruin my efforts. I made that list my first day at Cayucos for a reason; there's no turning back now. My claws are out, and my heels are dug in. No retreat, no surrender. I've already decided that I'll be taking the first opportunity at an early escape. I'll make an appearance and then run for it. Get out of there before the possibility of anything Blake should arise.

As soon as Dean finishes the episode that he was glued to on the Discovery channel, the three of us make a quick run to the grocery store. Marsha purchases an entire cart full of food so that she can put together a medley of chips and 'worthy dips.' As in freshly baked artichoke, seven layered beans, and my personal favorite -- a seaside bowl that's packed to the brim with miniature shrimp and southwest seasoning.

The artichoke dip has to be baked and then cooled fully, so it's bound to make us late. This is fine by me, as well as Dean and Marsha. They both refuse to be early to any kind of social gathering, especially ones where people are drinking and they've yet to meet the hosts.

"It's better to let everyone else get tipsy before you show up," Dean says before biting down on a grape from the bowl on the kitchen island.

Once the dips are all finished and the kitchen is cleaned, I retreat to the bathroom to freshen up and give myself a little pep talk in the mirror before going to Jacklyn and Tyler's house. The moon is nearly full and is beginning to rise, making both it and the sun visible in the darkening sky. Small waves crash against the sand. It crunches under my wedge shoes as we make the short walk to the neighboring condo.

Jacklyn and Tyler have done a beautiful job on their outside decor. The patio is large and sur-rounded completely with tiki lights, each a foot apart. The music is soothing. There's a wet bar over-looking the waves, with a table of food to each side of it. There's plenty of seating, most of it wrought iron with plush ocean-blue cushions on top. The only seating that isn't covered in softness are the rounded benches that circle a small fire pit on the corner of the patio, right as it lines the sandy beach. Best of all there are just enough people here that an early escape may just go unnoticed after all. As nice as it is to be out, making friends, I've dwelled on the fear of a run-in with Blake the man-boy far too long to let all reason fly out the window over a good time.

Tyler is tending to the barbeque and as we make our way into the small welcoming crowd, he waves me over. "Carla," he beams. "Glad you decided to come! I'm not supposed to tell you, but Jacklyn and I have had an open bet about it."

I chuckle and eye him suspiciously. "Who bet what?"

He quietly makes the notion of a zipper over his lips and then tosses his invisible key to the side. "This must be the twins that we've heard so much about?"

I introduce Dean and Marsha, who are as comfortable as can be. The first thing Dean notices is Tyler's Trojan's hat, which happens to be his favorite college football team. He even has the exact same one at home, which he now wishes he would have worn so that *they* could be the twinners. The two hit it off, like peas in a pod, talking about football and college aspirations. Tyler was once interested in the medical field but changed career paths shortly after starting college. Engineering comes naturally to him, so it wound up being a much better fit.

Marsha and I join Jacklyn and arrange our armloads of food on the empty spaces of her finger-food table. I munch on a few items, knowing that I'll be more satisfied after having left the party early, if I'd have tried out a few of the finger foods first. Jacklyn's aglow, the social break from life with newborn twins really is exactly what she needs, especially with her babies all safe and secure inside, being cared for by trusted loved ones. She takes Marsha and me around, introducing us to all of her friends and urging us to help ourselves to any food as well as the wet bar. Marsha opts for a light spritzer, only a splash of gin. I've brought my own beverage. Turns out that pineapple recipe was just the ticket; I've been hooked. But a little goes a long way, so I mixed my own tumbler to last me the duration of the night.

The small fire pit is calming, its flames dancing to the music, so I take a seat and engage in a small conversation with a lovely group of ladies swapping shopping tips. I'm soon up to speed on every upcoming shoe and handbag sale from here to LA. About twenty minutes into listening to an intent conversation about the use of fringe on bikinis between Marsha and a young woman with pixie blonde hair and six-inch stilettos, I glance across the patio. My gaze instantly locks on *his*. The world around me stills, as if time suddenly teeters the edge of nonexistence.

He doesn't blink, he doesn't smile or glare. He just stares, with a glint of wanting in his hungry eyes. He takes a sip of his beer without averting his gaze in the slightest, and I find myself mirroring his action. The cool pineapple zing that comes from my tumbler works its way down my throat, reminding me that even my beverage somehow revolves around the man that seems to be feasting on my soul through merely a look. The small circle of people around him continue to talk, unfazed by his lack of attention. Marsha, as she sits casually to my left, is a completely different story. The sound of her voice makes me gasp, granting my lungs the oxygen that I've deprived them for however long I've been staring back at... Blake.

"Wow, mom," she says and jolts me with her elbow. "Who's the babe?"

I continue to stare, our locked eyes remain intact, except now there are several more people looking in his direction due to Marsha's inquisitive nosiness. Blake smiles, obviously enjoying the sudden attention at my expense. Two gorgeously deep dimples sink into his cheeks and despite my seated position I can still feel my knees weaken. I squirm a little and clear my throat, still refusing to look away. If this is the game he wants to play, then so be it. The stubborn woman in me won't let me back down, especially now that I've sort of been made into a mockery. I can practically feel every woman around this fire pit staring back and forth between him and myself. I've been dreading the possibility of this moment for days, yet now that it's here I'm... *What am I? Enjoying it? Who are you, Carla?*

"Mom?" Marsha questions, her voice rising a tad bit with excitement.

I smirk, back at him, not at her and I pull my brows slightly together before I narrow my lids and tilt my head to the side. I'm not going to lose this little stare down to embarrassment. Not this time. I don't know these people, and I don't owe them any explanation. I lean toward Marsha and quietly try to pacify her. "I don't know who he is." I feed her a fraction of honesty. "We've never met."

"Hmmmm," she hums. I can only imagine the wheels in her head turning, and I don't want to imagine the conversation she'll be having with Dean later at my expense.

The pixie blonde breaks into the conversation. "That's Blake Aspen." She talks hushedly to Marsha, giving the rest of the women an irritated look, the subtle hint to go about their own business. I make a mental check note to thank her for the discreteness later, and I listen closely, my eyes still locked on his. "He lives a few condos down and practically every girl in Cayucos has been trying to nail him since his wife took off on a whim a few years ago."

"Hmmmm," Marsha repeats, the amusement

oozing from the coyness in her throaty voice. She nudges me again and begins quizzing her new friend. "And have any of these ladies succeeded?"

"Nope." The pixie haired woman straightens her back and grins. "He's like a vault. A playful, sexy, mysterious vault."

I think of the girl he'd thrown over his shoulder at the beach. She's must be one of the unsuccessfully hussies that he's oh so playful with. The thought makes me cringe.

"What happened with the wife?" Marsha continues to dig around.

"No one knows. They got married young, and she just took off. She doesn't have any family around here, so once she left, she never came back. For a while people speculated that her disappearance was an actual disappearance. You know, like the *real* kind. But she has a couple of friends who claim she calls them to check in here and there. They wouldn't say where she went, but according to law enforcement it doesn't matter. All they care about is that she was never actually missing."

"Weird," Marsha says pinching her face up tight.

"Blake, in the meantime," she continues to gossip quietly, "hasn't been with anyone since. She must have done a real number on him."

I continue to watch him as he finally breaks eye contact and throws an arm playfully around a young friend to his side. I take another sip of my depleting drink. It's running low way too early in the night, probably the reasoning behind my bravery. Nonetheless, it gives me more reason to stick with my plan of retreating to my condo the first chance I get. I refuse to give Marsha the satisfaction of further mockery. Instead I shake my head, more to myself than to her and I immediately squash the situation before it has a chance to turn into a bigger one.

"Well," I say matter-of-factly, "The women around here can keep trying for all I care." I clear my throat a second time and switch the cross of my thighs from my left to right leg on top, trying my best to regain an ounce of composure. "What were you saying about the two-piece you found at Zoe?"

Both of them instantly snap back to their previous conversation without missing a beat, but I'm not completely oblivious to the lingering looks coming from across the patio. The sun continues to lower beyond the shoreline, which heightens the tiki lights' illumination all around. Jacklyn soon takes a seat at my flank and passes around shots of tequila and sliced limes to toast in the summer. I gulp mine down with a cringe, allowing the heat of it to fill my throat before biting down on a lime to help wash the taste away. Without overthinking it, I hold out the shot glass for a quick refill. Maybe it'll loosen me up as Blake continues to consume my thoughts from across the way, his gorgeous blues stabbing into me like an ice pick with every sneaky glance.

I'm able to hold a light and upbeat conversation with Jacklyn and a small group of her increasingly tipsy friends for nearly an hour. The very last drop of my pineapple rum sloshes around the bottom of my tumbler, and I debate whether I can retreat completely without being noticed just yet. It's possible, as Dean and Marsha have now joined a moonlit game of beach volleyball. Blake is nowhere to be seen. Maybe he left too, without trying to talk to me. What a blessing that would be.

I lean toward Jacklyn and tell her just loud enough to be heard over the music. "When my kids are finished with their game, will you tell them I went back home to lay down? I'm not feeling well," I lie. "I think I had too much to drink, too fast."

Surprisingly, I'd love to stay and chat longer, but I can't bring myself to do it. The alcohol is kicking in and the lighthearted ambiance of the evening is making for an outstanding time. However, this may be my only opening for a smooth escape. I can't pass up the opportunity to get away, before my seeming admirer braves some sort of an encounter. My mind wanders to the look on his angry face the last time I'd witnessed him having too much to drink. In a strange way, the thought turns me on, and for a fleeting moment - *that* is what scares me.

"Are you sure?" Jacklyn quizzes with a speculative look in her eyes. "We're having such a fun time!"

"Yes," I insist. "Thank you so much for having me. If you need help cleaning up tomorrow, please let me know."

Jacklyn tells me that I'm welcome to come back if I catch a second wind, she's sure the guests will stay for a few hours longer, at least. I glance around again, making sure Blake is still nowhere to be seen, and I bolt for my exit. After ducking behind the wet bar, I slip off my shoes and trek across the sand barefoot. With a slight sway in my step, I nearly lose balance getting back onto my own patio. Luckily, I'm still fairly quick on my feet. I catch my balance, and then glance over my shoulder to make sure I haven't been followed. Paranoia is new for me, but after the piercing of Blake's sharp stare, I'm not surprised that it's made such an obtuse appearance.

Now that I'm home free I practically run for my bedroom door.

I suck in a long breath and place a hand over my heart before sliding my back down the wall and sitting on the floor. "What the hell, Carla?" I voice aloud and slap an open palm to my forehead. The thickly coated lashes that frame my closed eyes tickle my cheeks, and the slight tingling of my fingers remind me of what a wimp I really am. "This is horse shit," I say as I pull myself back up to a standing position. The hardwood beneath my feet is practically taunting me to stay with it. Come back, it beckons, you belong here. "No, Carla," I tell myself, "you don't belong on the fucking floor."

The music coming from Tyler and Jacklyn's place is cranked up a notch, and I can hear the beat of it through the screen of my opened bedroom windows. I smile and shake my head at my own secluded tenacity before retreating to the kitchen to pour myself another drink. There's a pitcher of the pineapple rum on the middle shelf. I help myself to two of the largest glasses I can find, and then I hide out in my room to watch television and wallow. It's only a matter of time before Dean and Marsha are blowing up my phone with text messages, checking in and calling me out on my bullshit.

A short, '*WTF mom. I know you're not sick,*' from Dean. Followed by a, '*That hot guy has been looking around, all frantic like. I'll bet he's lost without having you here to stare at,*' from Marsha. Followed by a quick second '*Maybe I'll go introduce myself. Tell him that you're home alone and looking for some company.*'

I roll my eyes and debate on a quick comeback, only to talk myself out of it. As far as they know I'm sleeping. She's bold, but not *that* bold. I call her bluff and leave it be. Two hours later, my twins bust through mud room doors. I listen to them giggle and try unsuccessfully to sneak around the kitchen for drunken bedtime snacks. I swing my feet off the bed, the start at a failing attempt to help them out. I didn't realize just how affected I am by the amount of alcohol I've had while sitting in bed, drinking and watching re-runs on television. My head spins, a darkness nearly consuming my vision, and I instantly sit back down. The music coming from the neighbors shuts off, and the last of the lingering voices disappear.

I stay seated on the edge of the bed and listen to my kids make their way around the condo. I wait a while. When everything stills and I'm confident they're passed out, I emerge from my pity-party. Much slower this time I stand, and on wobbly feet I check on Dean and Marsha. I pull a blanket over Marsha first as she's snoring loudly in Stephany's room, and then do the same for Dean on the couch. After having to place a hand on the wall in the hallway, and nearly losing my balance in the kitchen I opt for a lighter drink to take to the beach then more rum. Sleep isn't an option, not tonight.

$\mathcal{W}$ITH A SIX pack of spritzer and my feet as bare as they were the day I was born, I exit from the bedroom and walk to the water line. It's a few minutes past two in the morning and all of the neighbors' guests have gone. Everything is quiet aside from the soothing crash of waves against the shore. I chug one of my drinks, place it back into the empty slot it came out of and grab a second. At this point, I can hardly hold myself upright and I have no idea why I'm out here. Only that I can't sleep, and every time I close my eyes, I see his face.

I take a step into the welcoming water and it's cool. The relieving pulse of each depleting wave slaps up against my ankles. It feels good - too good not to want more. I glance around myself, checking each home along the beachfront. Sure enough, all the lights are out. Everything looks safe and quiet, so I set down the remainder of my drinks and slip off my dress. With one swift toss, I chuck it back far enough behind me that it'll stay safe and dry. My skin is instantly covered in goosebumps and the rush of standing alone, under the shadowy light of the night's sky, fills my blood with a rush of adrenaline. I walk into the water as if in a trance. I drop my head back and stare into the stars, allowing the rib-deep water to sway my relaxing body, back and forth with each petite wave. The salty scent fills my nostrils. I wiggle my toes until they sink a little, grounding me in place.

For the first time tonight I'm at peace, relaxed and feeling safe in the ocean, until the sound of crunching steps pulls me out of my trance. I spin around to see none other than Blake Aspen taking slow, calculated steps toward me. He's closing in the distance at a quick yet seemingly comfortable pace. Rather than running to the shore for my clothing, I find myself frozen in place. Like a statue, I'm stiff on the outside, unable to move. He stops at my dress, glances down at it and the back up at me. My top half is exposed, and in this moment, I couldn't be any more proud of myself for all the days I've spent killing myself at the gym - also for my choice of black lace bra and panties. I force myself to take a breath, and I watch him with my heart nearly racing away from my body.

He shoves his hands in his pockets, and I open my mouth to speak. I want to shout at him, ask him what the hell he is doing out here, if he followed me. Nothing comes out but an awkwardly wanting breath. It's as if the man has his own vibration, a unique spell of sorts that's causing my knees to weaken and my voice to falter. He's shirtless and shoeless. Call me crazy but the rise and fall of his chest is pulling me into his essence, like a spell. *It's got to be the alcohol.*

As I stand there, like a deer in the headlights, he does the unthinkable. Rather than talking or asking me why I'm nearly nude in the ocean in the middle of the night, he does something I never saw coming. Slowly, hesitantly, he pulls off his shorts. There's nothing underneath, so he places a hand over his member. *Down boy*, I think in my head. The embarrassing thought makes me chuckle to myself. I lower my head and place my hand like a shield in front of it. Much like one would if they were blocking out the sun. My other arm wraps firmly around my stomach. Before I know it, he's close.

"Carla," his voice is smooth and deep and only inches from me. The mere sound of it causes my goosebumps to return and a shutter to work its way up my spine.

I finally find my voice, and half shout, "I'm too old for a man-boy." Then I shake my head at myself. Of all the things to say, it had to be that.

"What?" he chuckles.

My eyes are still shielded, even though he's now in the water waist deep, barely covering his sensitive parts, and I can't see anything but his upper half. My chest is level with his stomach. I didn't realize how much bigger than me he really is, all this watching from a distance didn't do his powerful stature any justice. I lift my palm enough to spy up his abs and I nearly waffle, so I stop there and resume my hand's position before my sight gets to his face. I don't think I can hold my composure if we lock eyes again. Not at such close range. He's close enough for me to feel the heat of his body, and his scent... oh my. I don't answer or say anything else. I probably couldn't even if I tried.

"Carla," he says my name again, only softer, his voice hardly louder than the soothing sounds of the water around us. He takes another step forward, closing what little space was left in the gap between us. Our bodies are as close as you can get without actually touching. I hold my breath. "If I ask you a question, do you promise me an honest answer?"

I nod, bite down on my bottom lip and drop my hand away from my face. I keep my eyes closed tightly. I still can't look. I won't lie, I'll tell him anything he wants to know, but the anticipation of whatever he's so curious about causes my already rapidly beating heart to kick up a notch. I question its ability to stay pumping, and not stall out at the continuation of his voice.

"What do you want from me?" he asks quietly. If I didn't know any better, I would have detected a hint of begging behind his words.

That wasn't at all what I expected. I don't need to think about it though. In lieu of the honesty he asked for, I say, "Only to figure out why I'm drawn to you, I guess." I squeeze my lids shut even more.

Blake softly cups my face with both hands and pulls it up gently. "Open your eyes," he demands. I comply, and the instant they snap open I suck in a soul-reviving breath. Up close, his face is more defined and despite the sharp curve of his jaw his eyes are melted into a look of kindness. The blue of them seem brighter than before. He lowers his head closer to mine until our mouths are nearly touching. He stares at my bottom lip, as it's likely swollen from being chewed on. His own mouth opens slightly allowing him to breath me in.

I hesitate, yet before I lose my voice and my courage completely, giving into an animalistic urge to throw myself onto a stranger, I ask, "Why are you out here? Why me? There are plenty of other women around here. Younger, more beau..."

Before I can finish, he cuts me off by placing a palm over my mouth. I pull my brows together and glare at him angrily, but I don't reach up to pull him away. I'm not sure why either, I just stand there and let him cover my mouth to shush me, like a small child.

"I'm drawn to you, too." he says, his shoulders lowering a bit in surrender. "There is no one more beautiful, and I don't want you to say things like that." His brows lower as well, only in warning. He's upset at me, and I'm reminded of the broken bottle. I shrug but nod a slight understanding and he drops his palm. Surprisingly, he groans, loudly and fists his hairline, running his hands from his forehead all the way back to the base of his neck in frustration.

"Look," he levels with me. "I don't know what it is about you, but there's something. I've spent the last four years avoiding women, yet here I am, naked in the ocean with one that I don't even know. I don't date, I don't screw around. I'm not what you think I am, Carla."

"Who are you then?" I ask and cross my arms across my chest.

"I'm just a guy, in the water," he chuckles again, somehow conjuring back a lighthearted spirit, only this time I'm looking right at him.

The dimples make their appearance. I melt a little and drop my arms back down to my sides. His face levels and he takes another step closer; close enough for my breasts to touch him, but only my breasts. The rest of my body can feel every ounce of him from a short distance. His heat, his vibration, the up and down movement in his chest. I want to push myself against him. My nipples harden at the brushing touch. He reaches behind me and unclasps my bra, without unlocking eyes. Then he pulls the fabric away from my chest and slides it off of my arms before giving it a toss onto shore. He's eyes don't move from my face, nor does the intensity of them lessen.

With the softest of touches, he brushes his finger across my lips, and then moves it over my jaw, down my neckline and fingers the shape of my collar bone before stopping between my breasts. He lingers there and continues to stare. I'm trying my best not to pant at his touch, but the way he can raise the temperature of my entire body with one finger is quite possibly the most intimate experience I've ever had. Bradley never had this kind of effect on me. A sensation pools in the pit of my stomach and my inner thighs begin to ache as he continues to move his finger down my body. He stops at my navel before bending down at the middle and lowering his forehead to mine. I'm surprised to feel that his own breath is just as heavy as mine, and the realization of how close I am to sleeping with him slams into me like a semi.

I place my hand on his and pull it away. "I..I.. I can't do this," I stutter.

"Me either," he breathes before pressing his lips softly against mine.

My legs weaken and I have no choice but to grab onto his arms for balance. His kiss is soft, welcoming. I part my lips and let our tongues slide into rhythm. A quiet, irresistibly deep moan sounds from some place in the back of his throat. I take that as my cue. I'm drunk, and too old for this, no matter how irresistible he is. I peel myself away from him and storm off toward the shore. I can hear him groan and mumble be-hind me, but I refuse to look back. I half expect him to take a firm grip on my wrist and pull me back toward him. I want it, yet I don't want it, all at the same time. I don't know what I want, but I do know that a one-night stand with a sexy guy who's too young for me really isn't it... is it?

Before I know it, I'm snatching up my bra and dress that are shamelessly splayed out across the sand a few feet apart from each other and speed walking back to the condo to safety. I lock the door behind myself and jump straight into the shower to cool off. I get little to no sleep, tossing and turning all night. Oddly, I don't feel disturbed, or used or even dirty. Quite the oppo-site, really. For the first time in, well, ever probably, I feel genuinely wanted, desired, hungered for, even sexy. Until the sun comes back up in the morning, be-tween dozing off and waking up in cold sweats, I ques-tion my sanity. At one point I even consider jumping out of bed and marching straight to his house. I don't even think I'd say anything. I'd probably just pound on the door until he opened it and then throw myself at him the very second I got inside. Would I dare though?

Marsha is the first one out of bed in the morning, and she's found the bacon, hash browns and eggs in the fridge. By the time I drag myself down the hall, the two of them have eaten and are watching car-toons. No hangovers to behold, apparently. Jerks. I choke down a few bites of food off of the plate Marsha had left me in the microwave before cleaning up. It nearly comes back up, but I'm able to will the need to puke away. Mind over matter, I repeat in my head.

Dean joins me at the kitchen table. He leans his

body weight onto his elbows and stares with a goofy grin. "I don't get it." He says.

"Don't get what?" I ask as I swallow a few reheated hash browns down my throat with a heavy gulp. Then I wash it down with both water and coffee, just to be safe.

"How you can sleep in so late and have a hangover when you left the party so early." He lifts a brow and tilts his head to the side.

Marsha shouts from the other room. "Yeah, Mom!" They both chuckle. "What did you really do last night?"

My weak stomach sinks and I slide the plate away from me. "What are you weirdos talking about? I came back here and went to bed. I have a hangover because I'm no longer in my prime, remember?" I think of Blake's naked body next to mine in the ocean, and of the taste of his warm mouth. An icy chill creeps down the whole of my body. Surely, they can't know anything about my going out while they were sleeping... can they?

Marsha joins us at the table. Now they're both wide-eyed and leaning in to hear some juicy confession. Dean says, "Mom, we're adults, just spit it out. That Blake guy left at about the same time you did; Marsha saw him go after you."

"Yeah," Marsha continues for him. "Then, you didn't get up and talk to us when we came in. You always do, no matter how late it is. You didn't last night though, you just holed up in your room."

"Yep!" It's now back to Dean, his grin expanding. "And I woke up to the sound of your shower in the middle of the night."

"So, tell us, Mom." Marsha keeps at it. "Did you sneak that hot young guy past us last night?"

I glare at them both. My mind is reeling. If they only knew what really went down. My god, how embarrassing, and did Marsha just say that he left when I did? I guess her text really was a bluff. Was he watching me, waiting for hours in case I came back out? Couldn't have, that's crazy.

"For your information, I was alone here, and I tried to get up when you came but actually didn't feel well." I smile at them, knowing full well they can tell I'm being honest.

"Hmmmm," they both hum, drumming their fingers in unison. Dean blurts, "What was with the shower then?"

I choke on my coffee and cough into my fist. "When I shower is none of your business." I look at Marsha. "Yours either. I couldn't sleep and I was sick. Now go back to your cartoons and leave this old lady to her hangover in peace."

I sigh a breath of relief when it appears they've fallen for my bologna. Then I lean back in my chair and sip on my beverages. Alternating the coffee and water like a sickly animal, nursing myself back to health. Once we're past the hidden truths and omitting naked moments, we're right on track with everything normal and expected. I'm glad that they had such a great time with Jacklyn and Tyler. I make a mental note to invite them out with us the next time Marsha and Dean come to visit. I still have a couple months here, so they'll likely make the most of it and insist on coming here as often as summer classes permit, rather than me coming home.

The rest of the weekend is relaxing and quite perfect, really. Marsha and Dean cook all my meals and insist that I nap off my hangover. Everything is quiet, and aside from the two of them enjoying the beach, soaking up and having an occasional game of frisbee with Tyler and Jacklyn when they happen to be out in the sweltering heat at the same time, we mostly stay in. I choose to stay inside the most, mainly because I don't want to see Blake Aspen. I've avoided my back-yard beach for a reason, and that reason has intensi-fied rather than dissipated. I even catch myself spying out the window to make sure he isn't talking to my kids at any point. To my relief, it doesn't happen.

The two leave for home Sunday evening. It doesn't take long for my loneliness to return, and the quiet to remind me of what happened in the water. As the heat of the day sinks with the lowering sun, I choose a new book from the office library. This time my game of Spin-the-Carla lands on blue. The selec-tion is large, and making a choice isn't easy. I wind up settling for *The Lovely Bones* by Alice Sebold. I'm re-luctant to read a paranormal, as I'm all alone and have yet to read this genre since I got here, but this book has been on my to read list for far too long. Marsha has tried talking me into watching the movie with her and I've refused until I read the book. She'll be glad that I'll finally be willing to watch it.

I make myself comfortable on the patio and dive in. Page thirty-four is as far as I make it before none other than Blake himself decides to grace me with his presence. My heart thumps harder than usual, and I try my best to ignore him. He pulls the reclining chair that's identical to mine until he's close enough for me to smell his cologne. It's fresh, rustic. I like it. I swallow the lump in my throat and turn my page, pretending to read but am now completely unable. He leans the chair back and latches it, so that it's the exact same position as mine. Then he slides it over until they are touching, like a bed, and jumps on to join me.

I sigh, irritated, and turn a little to face him. "I'm reading, do you mind?"

"Shhh," he says, holding a finger into the air to shush me. He reaches into his deep cargo pocket and struggles a book out of it. A compact paperback copy of *The Great Gatsby* was shoved so tightly into the pocket that it didn't want to come out and the edges are all crinkled. It doesn't go unnoticed that the cover is blue. Nearly even the same shade as my own book. "Me too," he says and finds his place.

"You got to be shitting me," I mumble, and go back to pretending to read.

I turn pages randomly, here and there, for about ten minutes until I can't take it anymore. I slam my book onto my lap, raise the top half of my chair up a few inches, and then turn to him.

"How did you know I would be out here?" I demand.

"I've been watching you since you came to town," he replies, cool and calmly, without even looking up from his book. His breath remains level and he flip a page.

"That's quite the confession for being so calm," I say.

"I have nothing to hide from you, Carla," he replies and finally sets his book down. He interlocks his fingers behind his head, waiting confidently for more questions to shoot in his direction.

I comply, ready to fire at will. "The other night

you asked me what I wanted from you. Why would you ask me that?"

"I see the way you stare at me, and I know that you're just as pulled to me as I am to you. I can't figure it out really, but I'm willing to try. I guess I was curious, I want to know if you have an agenda."

I huff, "An agenda..." It's a statement, not a question. I lean back, and interlock my hands, mirroring him. If only it was an agenda. A goal, or a mission of sorts to hook up with a younger man while living on the beach. Now that would be understandable, commendable even for bravery and confidence. But whatever this really is, is just confusing, embarrassing, and ridiculous.

"So, tell me, Blake Aspen, what is *your* agenda?" I drag out *your*, my best effort to turn the tables on him for a change.

"It's not an agenda you should worry about." he says confidently, yet with a serious stare into the ocean front.

"Is there anything I should worry about?"

Blake stands, slides his chair about a foot away from my own so that he can sit back down facing me, with his legs between us. He leans forward onto them with his elbows on his knees. With a level face, and the stillness in his gaze he says, "Yes. You should worry more about my possessive, obsessive, and even demanding ways than you ever should an agenda. Like I said, I have nothing to hide from you, Carla. I have not been with any woman since my wife took off. I haven't wanted to, either. She took something from me, and I've had no time for women or nonsense until I get it back. That is, until you came along."

I lean forward and fidget with the hem of my sundress. I'm a little hesitant to ask, but a question is eating at me, gnawing away at my insides. I know that I should be more worried about his confession about being possessive and obsessive and even demanding, but it's the later part of his words that have me on edge. There's a pain behind his eyes, and for some reason it's being passed onto me. I can feel his heartache, and I'm not sure how to take it. "What did she take?" I whisper.

"That, I won't tell you. Not yet. Not until you're mine."

"Yours?" I chuckle. I can't help it. "What makes you think I'll ever be yours?"

His face remains just as level and serious as it had when he said the word possessive. His eyes seem to have sparked to life with the question. I gulp and he speaks. "I get what I want, Carla. At first, I was curious and even confused. But, since the other night happened, everything changed. I know what I want... that simple."

I can't seem to find my voice, and the small fidget of my fingers has progressed into a full-on kneading of the material of my dress. He leans forward and plants a small peck on my forehead before standing up and moving his chair back to its original place. "Oh," he says, and spins on his heels. "That hotel gym room is always empty. My sister's best friend works the front desk, and I work out for free. I've seen the way a few guys at the gym watch you, and I won't have it. I'll pick you up at eight and you can work out with me."

"You mean the girl you went to the beach with, and threw over your shoulder like a ragdoll?" The snarky acquisition bursts out of my mouth unexpectedly and catches even me by surprise. I cringe at myself, and bite down on both lips.

"Yeah, that was for you," Blake smiles his perfect tooth grin. "I saw you coming a mile away. Eight o'clock and wear those black yoga pants with the cherry blooms up the sides. They're my favorite."

I watch him walk away with my jaw dropped. He really has been watching me, close enough to know the exact time I always leave for the gym, to have my clothing memorized, and even to know who watches me when I work out. The logical side of my mind is screaming at me to run for the hills, but the sensual side is begging me to let him in. I'm torn in two directions and after watching him like a hawk until his powerful silhouette disappears in the distance, I snatch up my book and do my best to pick up where I left off.

Eight o'clock rolls around fast and I find myself pacing the front room in my yoga pants with the cherry blooms up the sides. Why am I allowing myself to go with this guy? I'm starting to question my sanity, but I've decided what the hell. He's right, there is something pulling us together and I'll be damned if I don't get to the bottom of it. There has to be something about him that turns me away, there's got to be, and I'm determined to find it. He's demanding, that clearly wasn't a lie, but I'm not worried about it in the slightest. If I didn't want to go, I wouldn't. I could care less about his demanding ways or his clear intent to own me in some strange possessive way. I'm not though. Curiosity trumps logic, and when he rings the doorbell right on cue, I practically run for it.

I stop myself at the handle and take in a deep breath to compose myself before swinging it open.

He's standing there, shirtless and in holey jeans that sag slightly from the downward pull of his hands in his pockets. Intentionally, I grind my teeth to keep my mouth from dropping open and then I twist my lips into a little smirk.

"Okay Mr. Demanding. Take me to this gym of yours." I march past him with a straight back and my head held high, our shoulders clip slightly. *Point one Carla*, I think and smile to myself while I climb into his Chevy pickup.

The ride is quiet, and it's all I can do to sit still and not squirm around in my seat. He's comfortable in the silence, which is completely fine by me. Chivalry isn't dead either, he opens the doors for me at the hotel, all of them. It's a nice gesture and it makes me feel kind of young again. Once we're in the gym, he sweeps an arm through the air. "Help yourself, I know you mostly run and use the pulleys, but if you want to use the free weights, I can help you and give you pointers."

I look up and scowl. "It's a little disturbing that you know my routine so well."

He only shrugs, "curious," he says.

I shake my head and storm off to the treadmill. I place my earbuds in my ears and find my favorite playlist before jumping on to run. I push myself more than usual, the decompression feels great. I steal little glances at my workout partner, who seems perfectly at home pushing his own limits. Whenever he catches me looking in his direction, he either smirks or winks. My legs nearly turn to noodles and I imagine myself slipping and the treadmill tossing my body at the wall behind me. The image makes me turn my head back and continue to avoid eye contact. The last thing I need is a trip to the hospital because I couldn't handle being watched by such a sexy man-boy. Point one, Blake. Damnit, we're all tied up.

We push ourselves for over an hour and as I wipe the sweat from my face and drink the last of my water, he's the first to call it a night. "It's getting dark," he says, "care for a swim?"

"Ha!" I half shout. "All I want right now is to shower and sleep. I'm exhausted. Don't count on anymore late night encounters any time soon. I only came to work out because you said it was free."

He smiles and gives me a nod. "Your wish is my command."

The ride back to the condo is just as quiet as the one to the hotel, only now I'm much more relaxed. The silence is nice, and I sink into it with ease. I take a deep breath, and I can very slightly catch a whiff of Blake's fresh sweat. A welcomed warmth fills my lower stomach and lean in his direction to take another deep breath. The motion is little yet doesn't go unnoticed. Blake places his left elbow on the rest between us and moves around in his seat so that he can lean my way too. I lay my head back onto the headrest and allow myself to melt into the comfort of the moment, of riding in a comfortable silence.

When Blake drops me off, he's a perfect gentleman. He doesn't say goodbye though, he says, "I'll see you tomorrow," and hurries off before I have a chance to interject.

I'm exhausted from the entire weekend and I sleep like a baby. The next morning, I'm not surprised to find Blake on my bedroom patio, halfway through *The Great Gatsby*. This time I join him, not the other way around. I decided on the same pineapple dress I had on the first time I came to Cayucos. With two glasses of pineapple rum -one for each of us - and my book in hand I make myself comfortable. I'm well aware that it's way too early to start drinking, especially rum in California's summer heat. We'll only stay out until it gets too hot, and I'll be damned if he joins me inside.

We sip our dinks and sink into comfort with our books. It feels natural and calming. In all the years I was married to Bradley, and in all the years I've been alone, I can't recall a time I was ever so comfortable. Just lying under the rising sun and burying myself into a book with the very soft yet distinct sound of a man's breath beside me. After a good hour or so, we begin to talk between the turning of pages. Small questions and answers. Short and sweet. When it begins growing too hot and my stomach rumbles, hinting around to be fed, Blake stands and walks away. Back to his own house, no goodbyes, no awkward moments.

He doesn't say anything about a workout on his way out. I don't ask, I only assume he'll be here to pick me up, and sure enough he doesn't disappoint. At eight o'clock exactly, he's knocking on the door. Things continue like this for an entire week. I learned that Blake Aspen inherited his condo as well as about half a million dollars when his parents passed away in a car accident. He was a teenager at the time and his girlfriend clung to him through the grief. He married her and a few years later, she ran away with several thousand dollars. He's merely twenty-eight years old yet holds the composure of a man who knows exactly what he wants and when. He doesn't say anything else about her taking something from him, and I don't ask. I can feel the pain seep through his words, and I decide he'll tell me if or when he's ever ready. Before, he said he wouldn't say until I'm his. I'm not ready for another comment like that, so I decide to let it slide.

After seven full days of falling into routine with Blake, he suddenly stops coming around. I don't know what I did or said to cause his sudden disinterest, but it's left me unsettled. I feel strangely empty, wandering around the condo like a pet who's lost her human. I debate on showing up on his doorstep just the same as he did mine, but I can't bring myself to do it. Day in and day out, I wait outside in the mornings. I go to the same gym I went to before Blake came along and push my body's limits even harder than usual. I'm angry and feel a weird sort of abandonment.

The following weekend my kids make another trip out, and I need their distraction from everything Blake Aspen more than I care to admit. It's a Friday afternoon and I look through the peephole to see Marsha and Dean, standing on the porch grinning from ear to ear, wholly proud of themselves for the surprise of being early. I swing the door open and the three of us squeal. Marsha reaches over to the wicker chair on the porch and picks up a bouquet of roses.

"Did you know this was here?" She smiles and cocks her head to the side, raising an eyebrow in my direction. "Looks like you have an admirer!"

Dean snatches it from her hands and marches past us both to the kitchen. "It's him isn't it? That Blake guy from the barbeque. It's been a couple weeks, are you dating him?" He wags his eyebrows at me in approval.

Marsha and I follow him, nearly clipping his heels on the way. I grab the flowers the second he sets them down on the counter. Dean fetches a couple waters from the fridge and hands one to Marsha. They each take a guzzle and I chuckle at them. "Thirsty?" I tease.

Marsha tilts her head back and gives a satisfactory groan, "Ahhh. We left our drinks at home and didn't want to stop. We drove on through with nothing but the gum and candy bar that I had stashed in my purse."

I fetch a vase to put my flowers in and as I pull them out of their wrapping a note falls out. The three of us scramble for it, each one trying to snatch it up before the other. We're all giggles and elbows for about three seconds. Of course, I win. Dean slams a fist of defeat on the counter and mumbles, "Damnit." Marsha folds her arms over her chest and pouts.

"Well," she says. "Are you going to read it out loud, or what?"

I look down and read it to myself first, throwing an open palm in the air to stop Dean and he tries to walk around me and read it over my shoulder. It says:

Carla,

I've decided to stop visiting you. I need more. Meet me after dark on the shoreline so I can pick up where I left off. So I can do all the things I haven't stopped thinking about since I saw you naked. I'll wait every night, for as long as it takes.

– Yours, Blake

I CAN FEEL my cheeks darken, and the space between my upper thighs stir.

"Well?" Marsha demands, arms still folded across herself.

"It's none of your business," I say precisely, before walking to the garbage and ripping the note into a million tiny pieces so that my nosy kids can't find and read it later. "It doesn't really matter anyway. We're not dating, I haven't been with him, and he's too young."

Both of my kids stare at me, like statues holding their breath. I stare back for a moment. "What?!" I finally shout, well aware of the still ever-darkening shade of my cheeks and ears. To that, they both double over in laughter. Marsha dumps her head into her folded arms on the counter, and an adorable snort sounds from within. Dean pretends to wipe a funny tear from his eyes.

"Whatever, Mom," they both say in unison, reading me like an open book.

We play card games and gorge ourselves on way too much popcorn and ice cream while binge-watching *The Walking Dead* for the thousandth time. As soon as Marsha and Dean call it a night and are fast asleep, I quietly sneak out. I know that I shouldn't be caving into his request, but I'm pulled to him. I've missed him and am willing to see where the night takes me. My hands are shaking, and my legs struggle to carry me to him.

I find Blake sitting in the sand with his forehead dumped into the palms of his hands. There's a large manilla envelope sitting in his lap, and as soon as I sit next to him, I can smell the liquor on his breath.

"Blake?" I hesitate but lean my head around him

to find his eyes with my own. They're bloodshot from tears, and his fists clench at the sound of my saying his name.

I'm suddenly afraid, and I consider running back to the condo and forever locking the door.

"Do you remember when you asked me what she took?" He asks with a wildly scratchy voice.

"Yeess," I draw it out, unknowing if I can handle what may come next.

"I've spent it all. Every dime trying to find her, and here it is." He shakes the envelope around in the air. "They finally tracked her down." His voice cracks and he sniffles the loose snot in his nose.

"You told me you wouldn't tell me until I was yours," I remind him quietly.

He turns to me and grabs my face in both of his hands. Roughly he presses his lips against mine and pushes his tongue in. It's intense and wanting, but I welcome it and return the passion of his kiss. I pull up the sides of my sundress and straddle him, the sand clinging to the bottom half of my legs. I pull away from the kiss and look into his eyes.

"What is in the envelope?" I ask.

He hands me the envelope and wraps his arms around my waist. While he cries into my chest, I open the envelope behind his back and pull out a stack of photos.

My stomach sinks and twists.

One still shot after another; I flip through the images. They all have a scrawny, sickly-looking woman, around Blake's age, with her eyes sunken in and her teeth half-missing. She laughs and jokes around with several men on a holey couch. To the side of the couch is a young girl, no older than five years. A thick circle with permanent marker frames her in every picture. She's playing cards on a dirty floor with a half-eaten sandwich and a giant floppy sun hat next to her. The polish on her toes is a bubblegum pink.

I gasp. "Is she... yours?" I whisper.

"Yes," he chokes. "The detective gave me the envelope today, after I left your flowers. I have to get her back, Carla. I have to find a way."

I hold him close and allow a flow of my own tears to escape my eyes. "I'm yours," I whisper, ready to help him find the young girl from my dream. The girl who felt like my own. The girl who called me C-ma. I place the photos back in their envelope, set it down with care on top of my towel and stand. His hands are warm inside of mine as I help pull him to his feet. He complies and follows me to the water.

Dear reader,

We hope you enjoyed reading *Skinny Dippin'*. Please take a moment to leave a review, even if it's a short one. Your opinion is important to us.

Discover more books by Didi Oviatt at https://www.nextchapter.pub/authors/didi-oviatt

Want to know when one of our books is free or discounted? Join the newsletter at http://eepurl.com/bqqB3H

Best Regards,

Didi Oviatt and the Next Chapter Team

You might also like:

Time Wasters by Didi Oviatt

To read the first chapter for free, please head to:
https://www.nextchapter.pub/books/time-wasters

ABOUT THE AUTHOR

Didi Oviatt is an intuitive soul. She's a wife and mother first, with one son and one daughter. Her thirst to write was developed at an early age, and she never looked back. After digging down deep and getting in touch with her literary self, she's writing mystery/thrillers like Search for Maylee, Justice for Belle, Aggravated Momentum, and Sketch, along with multiple short story collections. She's collaborated with Kim Knight in an ongoing interactive short story anthology, The Suspenseful Collection. Most recently, she published her first romance novella titled Skinny Dippin' which was originally released as a part of the highly appraised Anthology, Sinners and Saints, When Didi doesn't have her nose buried in a book, she can be found enjoying a laid-back outdoorsy lifestyle. Time spent sleeping under the stars, hiking, fishing, and ATVing the back roads of beautiful mountain trails, and sun-bathing in the desert heat play an important part of her day to day lifestyle.

Listen to Didi Oviatt's books on Audible:
https://www.audible.com/author/Didi-Oviatt/BooHVJJTLE

Where to find Didi:
https://didioviatt.wordpress.com

facebook.com/didioviatt

twitter.com/Didi_Oviatt

instagram.com/didioviatt

amazon.com/author/didioviatt

bookbub.com/authors/didi-oviatt

But who is the cold, calculated murderer, and can they find a way to survive?

Praise:

★★★★★ - "There is an authenticity to Ms. Oviatt's writing that is refreshing to experience in a thriller-type novel."

★★★★★ - "A murder mystery with plenty of drama, suspense and danger. Fans of mystery and thriller genres will love this book."

★★★★★ - "Fast-paced and full of twists I never saw coming. I was hooked immediately."

Justice for Belle: http://mybook.to/justiceforbelle

Ahnia has a very dicey past - one that is scratching under the surface, just dying to get out.

She's hit rock bottom, broke and desperate to be on top again. When she finds herself partnering up with a man she hardly knows, and who's utterly untouchable, she's forced out of her comfort zone in every way.

Will Ahnia and Mac's dangerous decision be a success, or will she find herself in the clutches of an unforgiving force, brought about by her childhood sin?

In this nail-biting thrill ride, no one is as they seem...and no one is truly safe with those they trust.

Sketch: http://mybook.to/sketch

When local girl Misty is found dead in an underground

bunker, the town is thrown into a whirlwind of panic and speculation. Times are tough, but the spaced-out farmer community pulls together as one, trying to uncover who's guilty.

Thrown smack in the middle of the chaos is a group of teens: local troublemakers, but with good hearts. Although they're innocent, the local law enforcers believe otherwise, and the true killer is lurking far too close for comfort.

Will the four be able to uncover the truth before one of them pays the price for Misty's death?

~

THE SUSPENSEFUL COLLECTION (VOL. 1): FOR MATURE READERS ONLY:

A suspenseful novel with a twist. Eight short stories, by two suspense authors, from diverse backgrounds. From opposite sides of the Atlantic these stories have been created. One author started the tale and the other ended it. No discussion, no pre-planning, but yet their stories are seamless. With just creativity and the use of writing prompts, to craft one tale, with two different writers. This anthology of suspenseful, fast paced and engaging tales covers multiple genres. From heart felt romance, crime, fantasy, and steamy historical fiction. There is a story for everyone!

Steamy Historical Crime Fiction: It was The First Time I Killed A Man.

It's 1972 and New York's first female serial killer Lisa Vanacilli is in the hot seat again, ten years after her conviction of murder to the first degree and innocent plea. The ruthless but sexy reporter Tiffany Low cracks Lisa for a confession... at a price. Lisa is strong, courageous and says it how it is. This story has been extended due to reader's demand. And is only for adult readers.

Psychological Fiction: Every Time I Hear That Voice From The Basement.

George appears to be harmless. The local neighbourhood geek on the outside, married to Jolene. In reality, he's a very disturbed man. His path crosses with Dana, the local check out girl. This is a psychological suspense story with a twist.

Crime Fiction: The Entrance To The Tunnel Is His Only Way Out.

Juan is a wanted man, and an ex-gang member on the run from Atlanta to Mexico. With a hundred grand in cash stolen from his ex-boss, he meets an unlikely fate in Mexico. A fast-paced crime fiction story.

Contemporary Romance: When His Hands Run Up My Thighs I...

Love has no time limit, age limit or use by date. Sarah now in her fifties is reunited with her long-lost love Joshua. They last had contact in 1961. In the present day, thanks to the advancement of technology their paths cross. A heart-warming and modern tale, about long distance love, that will leave you warm inside.

Suspense: We Only Said Goodbye With Words, I Died A Hundred Times:

In 1963 Russian Femme Fatale Mila Petrov is London's top Madam. Her entertainment house is booming, she has a team of London's strongest women behind her. Unfinished business from her past creeps up and haunts her. It's nothing she can't handle. A suspenseful historical tale, with a strong femme fatale.

Fantasy: The Ones Who Live At The Bottom Of The Ocean, Come To The Surface.

A beautiful coming of age story, featuring sixteen year old Zoe and her mother May-Li. Myth becomes reality, as Zoe finds out who and what she really is. Her mixed descent reveals more than what meets the eye. This fantasy story is set against the backdrop of a Greek island and Hong Kong, China.

Suspenseful Crime Fiction: Guilty As Charged, In Self-Defence

California's sassy, tough, and likeable defence lawyer Catherine has taken on a case so high profile, if she wins she'll become a partner of Martin Law Firm. Defending forty six year old Mrs. Chevelle. An ex Las Vegas show girl, now a Hollywood wife, on trial for the murder of her high-profile husband. She claims she's innocent. Readers are taken on a fast -paced journey on a mission to seek the truth.

Contemporary Fiction: It's A Man's Man's World:

A beautiful modern tale showing the love and appreciation of a woman. James Brown said it right when he said, "it's a man's man's world, but it would mean nothing without a woman or a girl."

BLURRED LINES (THE SUSPENSEFUL COLLECTION VOL. 2): FOR MATURE READERS ONLY:

As the second installment of suspenseful short stories by two suspense authors, from diverse backgrounds, Blurred Lines offers a thrill ride with nine stories in genres across the board. From opposite sides of the Atlantic these stories have been created. One author started the tale and the other ended it. No discussion, no pre-planning, but yet their stories are seamless. With the use of writing prompts Kim and Didi have created tales that will tug at your heart strings, drop your jaws, and leave you clinging to the edge of your seat. From gory horror, romance, crime fiction, family drama, and fantasy, there is a story for everyone!

Crime Fiction, Psychological: "I'm Back Bitches, Now Panic!"

Lynn McCarmick has spent six years behind bars for a crime she didn't commit, although she's a far cry from an innocent woman. Her once loyal team of con artists set her up for a robbery that landed her a long term home in a Scottish prison. After an early release for good behavior, Lynn is finally able to let the bad bitch inside of her roam free.

Contemporary Romance: Heart of Gold

In this star crossed, light hearted tale, two people with the purest of hearts, each long to find a mate who is giving, honest and real. A heart-felt romance.

Psychological Thriller, Slasher Romance, Erotica: Chainsaw Ridge

Alice is one of a kind, and was raised by a nasty man with killer habits. After an accident rendered the awful man disabled, everything changed. With an ultimate twist, this gory tale takes Alice and her husband on one hell of a bloody adventure. Due to popular demand this story was extended!

Investigative Crime Fiction: Crime Scene Investigation

Detectives Flynn and McBride are on the case of a murder. Owner of the Chinese restaurant where the body was found, Mr. Wang, is devastated. The pressure is on to find the killer and to clear Mr. Wang's establishment as a safe place for his patrons. The detectives piece together outside connections that are weaved into Mr. Wang's ties, in a very delicate way. Is there more to the murder than what meets the eye?

Historical Fiction: A Miracle Baby Story

In a tragic tale of tough love and loss, brought about in a western setting, two young lovers are frowned upon by nearly everyone around. Adsila is a teen of Cherokee descent, who falls for a young cowboy. In a bitter-sweet tale she fights for the survival of herself and unborn child in a community filled with hate and judgement.

Paranormal Suspense: A life Gone?

Franklyn Poppy, is a husband and father who found himself in a place between life and death. He becomes a loathly witness to the woman he loves having an affair with his twin brother. He's introduced to the infamous dark Goddess, Maman Bridgette who shares his disdain for the happenings with his wife. The outcome for Mrs. Poppy and her fateful intertwining with this powerful Goddess is powerful and resonating.

Metaphysics, Clairvoyant, Thriller: Murder by Mistake

The Wilkinson family consists of an Air Force father, a loving mother, and two daughters Anna and Julie. They are polar opposites, and Julie, the younger of the two has a special gift. She's able to see things before they happen. When she's mentally the witness to a murder that's yet to be solved, she's forced into action in an altercation with the killer.

Fantasy: Witchful Thinking

Gretchen isn't your average witch, as she was born into a

clan descending from the blood of Fate herself. Growing up in foster care was an intentional way for her to find her own path in using her magic, as she's intended to be a tool for Fate's use. A twisty tale set in the present and past day.

Family Drama: Real Mom

After the abandonment of their mother, twins Josephine and Jerilynn are taken in by their new stepmom, and become the big sisters to quite the large and quirky family. During a family vacation the two team up, and try to uncover the mystery of their estranged biological mom.

~

NEW AGE LAMIANS: HTTP://
MYBOOK.TO/NEWAGELAMIANS

Jackson has barely reached manhood when lightning heralds the end of the world as we know it. The lightning has awakened the Lamians: descendants of the mythological creature Lamia.

In his world, The Company delivers supplies into his village, and harnesses technology that others lack. Soon, Jackson is taken by The Company; he is to be an ultimate warrior, alongside few others, as their blood is rare and compatible with the technology needed to transform them.

According to The Company, the Lamians are monsters who need to be defeated at all costs. But is Jackson really the one who can save the world?

Praise:

★★★★★ - *"A twisty, intoxicating read."*

★★★★★ - *"Genuinely imaginative."*

★★★★★ - *"Compellingly entertaining"*

Skinny Dippin'
ISBN: 978-4-86750-113-9
Mass Market

Published by
Next Chapter
1-60-20 Minami-Otsuka
170-0005 Toshima-Ku, Tokyo
+818035793528

4th June 2021

9 784867 501139